The Phantom of Phys Ed

Look for these SpineChillers™

#1   *Dr. Shivers' Carnival*
#2   *Attack of the Killer House*
#3   *The Venom Versus Me*
#4   *Pizza with Extra Creeps*
#6   *Not a Creature Was Stirring?*

SPINE CHILLERS™

The Phantom
of Phys Ed

Fred E. Katz

Publishers Since 1798

THOMAS NELSON PUBLISHERS
Nashville • Atlanta • London • Vancouver

Published in Nashville, Tennessee, by Thomas Nelson, Inc., Publishers, and distributed in Canada by Word Communications, Ltd., Richmond, British Columbia. SpineChillers™ is a trademark of Thomas Nelson, Inc., Publishers.

Scriptures quoted from the *International Children's Bible, New Century Version,* copyright © 1983, 1986, 1988 by Word Publishing, Dallas, Texas 75039. Used by permission.

Editor: Lila Empson; Copyeditor: Dimples Kellogg; Packaging: Sabra Smith.

ISBN 0–7852–7497–9

Printed in the United States of America.

2 3 4 5 6—01 00 99 98 97 96

High-pitched screeches filled the air behind me, and earsplitting bellows rushed at me. I stood with my eyes wide and staring. Kids raced by me.

Standing on the front sidewalk of my new middle school, I stared at the old red-brick walls. A mixture of feelings ran through me as fast as the kids who ripped by.

I was still frozen in place when it sounded again. The final bell signaled the beginning of my first day at Crider Middle School.

We had moved from a big city to a small town in the Midwest because my brother, Ben, already had a job here as a librarian and Dad thought that raising a family in a small town would be ideal.

But now I was alone.

I was lost.

And I was a little frightened.

But I had to go in.

The stone steps leading up to the old-fashioned

wooden doors were worn from all the years and all the kids. I went as slowly as I could.

The halls were empty by the time I reached the entrance, and it was spooky. As I stepped inside, the high ceilings, old lockers, and linoleum floor worked together to make each step echo as if I was in a huge cave. I knew anyone listening would be thinking, *She must be that new girl.*

"That new girl" was exactly who I was. I didn't know anyone. I didn't like the idea of being looked at by everyone who already knew everyone else.

On top of being new, I was tall for my age. My height came in handy for the basketball team, but it made me stand out above the crowd. Literally. Especially when I was trying to melt into the wall.

I stopped in front of the school's office and sucked in a breath. As I reached for the doorknob, the door flew open in front of me, but I didn't see anyone on the other side. What happened?

Cautiously, I stepped through the doorway and into the office. With a small, quiet shuffle I made my way toward the office counter.

Several women and men moved in a flurry of activity from one desk to another. No one noticed me. That was good. Not every person in the school would be staring at me.

Suddenly, the door crashed shut behind me. I turned to face a tall, thick man with hair that stuck straight up in the air. His nose was large and hooked. His arms were so long that they nearly reached his knees.

If he hadn't been between me and the door, I would have been out of there and home in three seconds.

He reached a long, bony-fingered hand toward me and said to the milling faculty, "Ladies and gentlemen of the Crider Middle School staff, I would like you to meet our newest student, Caitlin James."

Every eye and head was fixed on me. I felt like a fish in the first-grade aquarium—everyone's eyes were so close that I could see myself in every one of them.

"Welcome, Caitlin," the staff said in unison as their faces lit up with smiles.

I tried to say "Hi," but my mouth was so dry that only the *i* came out in a high-pitched whistle. My face turned red. All I wanted to do was race out of there and not come back.

But the tall man was between me and the door. So I cleared my throat and tried it again: "Hello." It came out fine that time, and I relaxed. It was a lot easier for me to sing in front of other people than it was to talk.

"We have been expecting you. We all know how difficult it is at a new school on the first day, so we wanted to make it easy for you. Come into my office and I'll tell you about your day."

3

I followed him into his office—the principal's office. That was my first clue that he must be Dr. Wiser. He spent the next few minutes shoving papers into my hands and explaining my schedule to me.

When he finished, I asked about the topic dear to my heart. "Dr. Wiser, can I still try out for the basketball team?"

"Caitlin, Coach Fancher is expecting you after school. I hope you brought your practice clothes."

"Right in my bag," I said as I lifted my gym bag off the floor.

"I think you already know that we don't have separate girls' and boys' basketball teams—our team is coed. Three other girls are on the team. From what I hear about your ability, you may end up being our star player," the principal informed me.

In the last school, I was the leading scorer in our division. Being tall for my age was great on the basketball court. The court was where I did my best work, but this would be my first official coed team.

Dr. Wiser's voice snapped me back from my school daze. "Caitlin, let me show you to your locker." We got up and headed out the door and down the cavernous hallway as he talked softly in a voice most people reserve for the library.

"Since the school is so old, we barely have enough lockers for students. In the past, some kids have even shared lockers. The good news is that there is

4

one locker left. The bad news is that it is in the farthest, most out-of-the-way place."

We walked around several corners and eventually got to a short corridor. I headed back toward the end with Dr. Wiser. The farther in we got, the worse it smelled.

I kept gagging with each step until we could go no farther.

Two lockers stood next to each other at the end of the hall. No wonder my locker was still empty. The one next to it smelled like rotten eggs mixed with old, sweaty gym clothes. Green goo oozed from its vents.

2

"Dr. Wiser, what's that smell?"

"Hmm. Your locker is the one on the right. This one next to yours," he said as his hand went near the left one but did not touch it, "doesn't seem to be currently habitable."

"You can say that again," I told him as I tossed my bag into my locker and backed out of the small corridor as fast as I could.

Dr. Wiser spent the rest of the morning showing me around the school. By the time we finished, I actually knew where everything was and some of the shortcuts through the halls.

At lunchtime he dropped me off at the cafeteria and pointed out a table of kids. He told me that they were waiting to meet me after I bought my lunch. The cafeteria food smelled good compared to the stinky locker that had so recently attacked my nose.

I was grateful to see some faces that smiled at me as I guided my tray with mystery meat, shriveled green beans, and a hard-as-rock peanut butter cookie back to their table.

"Hi, I'm Scott. Dr. Wiser said that you would be arriving here today. We're really glad to have you at Crider Middle School. How's your first day going?"

Scott was a pretty neat kid, and he lived only a block from our new house.

"Hi, I'm Iza," a girl with dark, curly hair that tumbled down to her shoulders said. She had a really big smile.

"Iza? That's kind of a strange name," I told her.

"Well, it's short for Isabella. Iza is a whole lot easier for my friends to remember. And this is Kris," Iza said as she pointed toward the blonde, blue-eyed girl next to her.

Kris made Iza's hair look darker, and Iza made Kris's complexion look lighter. As different as the two of them looked, that was how similar they acted. Both of them were crazy.

Kris extended her hand and I gave her five. I liked those three already.

Iza put a paper bag on the table and pulled out a plump, yellowish red fruit. "Look what I found at the grocery store. It's the rage in Florida. I thought we could try something different."

As Iza sliced the mango, Scott slid around on the cafeteria bench. He was filled with questions. "So where did you move from?"

"My family lived in a suburb of Metro City. I think I'll miss all the activity of a big city—at least for a while. We were members of a large church that had lots of youth activities. I sang soprano in the youth choir.

"And I miss having a mall down the street from our house," I told them.

"You had a mall down the street from your house?" Iza exclaimed.

"Why in the world would your parents want to move here from a house so close to a mall? From here you have to drive over a half hour to reach one. And there aren't many stores in this town. You don't get much smaller than we are here. My uncle always jokes that if you blink while driving down Main Street, you'll miss the town," Kris added.

Kris and Scott helped themselves to the mango slices. Iza invited me to help myself too. "Have some, Caitlin. It's the sweetest stuff I've ever eaten." She was right. I ate a few more pieces as we talked.

Scott had another question. "What kind of things do you like to do?"

"Basketball is my favorite," I said with a beaming face.

"Great. Maybe you can help us win the championship this year," Scott said. "Do you have any questions for us?"

"Not really. Dr. Wiser was rather thorough. I think

that I know the whole school setup now. He told me about everything but one small item." I quizzically bent my eyebrows as I said it.

"Fire away. What do you need to know?" Kris inquired.

"Dr. Wiser told me that I got the last available locker, but it is right next to the stinkiest locker I have ever sniffed. It had green goo dripping out of the vents too," I told them.

You would have thought that I told them something horrible. They sat there frozen. Not one of the three moved so much as an eyelash. "Is everything all right?" I asked.

Scott was speechless for another few seconds, which surprised me. Then he blurted out, "Your locker is next to Hezekiah Bones's locker."

"Who is he? And why doesn't he clean it out?" I asked the others indignantly.

"Hezekiah Bones disappeared more than fifty years ago, and his locker has been sealed ever since. There's supposed to be a horrible curse on that locker. If you so much as touch it . . ." Scott was explaining just as the bell ending lunch sounded.

My mouth was wide open. "What? What happens if you touch it?"

"You become cursed," he whispered.

9

"I've got to get to my next class, but you're in my study hall so I'll finish telling you in there. But don't touch the locker under any circumstances. Promise me that you won't touch it," he warned in a very serious voice.

"Okay, I promise. I won't touch it. But why?" I questioned, but my query didn't reach his ears.

Scott was already racing away from me and down the hall. I put the tray on the conveyor belt and walked slowly to my next class. It was English and following that was study hall.

I was barely able to keep my mind on what the teacher was saying. Of course, she kept looking at me to make sure that I understood all that she was explaining. I think my smiles convinced her that I wasn't in some dreamland.

The truth was that all I could think of was Hezekiah Bones, the smelly locker, and the curse. How could people get cursed by just touching the locker? I believed in Jesus and knew he would protect me. So I wasn't usually scared by such things. Still, the idea was pretty spooky, and I didn't care to spend the rest of the school year next to a smelly locker. Nobody had to tell *me* not to touch it!

When the bell rang, I was through the doorway before the other kids could even rise from their chairs. I checked in with the teacher monitoring study hall. It really wasn't a great room to study in. It was the school's auditorium.

My eyes roamed over the rows of seats for Scott's face. I didn't see him. All I saw were brown theater seats wherever I looked.

At that point, I wasn't worried about trying to find a comfortable seat. I had a curse on my mind.

Suddenly, out of the corner of my eye, Scott entered the auditorium. I moved his way as he slid into an aisle seat.

I dropped into the seat next to him. "You've got to tell me about the curse," I demanded.

"Be quiet or the teacher will move you away from me. I'll tell you later," he whispered.

I sat tapping my foot until the teacher left. The moment his back was out of sight, I leaned near Scott and demanded, "Now! Tell me now!"

"Okay, I'll tell you, but I hear there is a curse on anyone who even tells the story. I'm probably going to get zapped somehow," he said with serious-looking eyebrows that bent low in the middle of his forehead.

"What kind of curse will you get?" I asked out of polite consideration for him.

"It isn't too bad. I become invisible for a day. No one can hear me or see me. Just think of all the trouble I can get into if I'm invisible," he told me as a mischievous grin grew across his face.

"Well, if you're not afraid of the curse, go ahead and tell me about Hezekiah Bones," I said.

"Of course I'm not afraid of the curse. Are you afraid of it?" he asked.

I swallowed hard. I didn't feel very good about it, that was for sure. I blurted out, "Me? Afraid of a curse? Ha! There's no such thing as a curse."

"That's what I used to think too. The locker that stands next to yours has been there for years and years, even before my parents went to school here."

I interrupted. "Why hasn't someone opened the locker?"

"No one can. They say that people have tried, but the moment someone touches the locker to open it, the curse strikes. Besides, no one knows what is in there. Some people say it's the skeleton of Hezekiah Bones, and others say it's his victims. I think his old, sweaty gym clothes are in there," Scott said.

"No one knows what's inside the locker?" I asked.

"Nope. Nobody has been in it at all since the day

that Hezekiah Bones disappeared from the gym floor during a basketball game," he answered.

My mouth was wide open as he continued. "Hezekiah Bones was the greatest middle school basketball player of all time. He was over six feet tall in the seventh grade, but like his last name, he was all bones.

"During the championship game, the Crider Cats were up by only one basket. There were only two minutes left in the game. Hezekiah went up for a rebound and landed hard on the gym floor. When he landed, he broke a shoestring.

"The coach asked for a time-out and sent Hezekiah Bones to the locker room to get a new shoestring. That was the last time anyone ever saw him alive.

"I don't know what happened to him. No one knows what happened. But we know that the spirit of Hezekiah Bones is supposed to roam our school searching for victims who touch his locker.

"If you touch it, you break out in a red itchy rash, weird things start happening to you, and he comes back and drags you into his locker to rot with everything else."

"That sounds really crazy," I scoffed.

"Yeah, I suppose so, but there is more to the story," Scott told me as he launched into the next part of the tale. "Hezekiah Bones has not been seen in the school, but there have been times when we all knew he was around."

13

I asked, "How did you know?"

"Wherever Hezekiah goes, a horrible smell follows him," Scott said as he settled back in his seat.

I sat next to him, stunned. My family had moved to a safe little town to get away from the big city influences, and I got plopped right down in the middle of a curse. This was not cool at all.

I tried to look at one of my books, but my mind stayed only on the curse of Hezekiah Bones. I was hearing Scott's words all over again in my head when I started to smell something.

Did Scott have his gym clothes with him?

Was someone in the next row eating Limburger cheese?

I didn't see a thing, but the smell was getting worse.

Suddenly, a guy started to gag. The girl next to him screamed that a poisonous gas was in the room.

Then I realized what it could be.

I looked nervously at Scott and he looked at me. "Hezekiah Bones?"

Scott looked pale. He could barely whisper, "He's coming after me!"

The teacher raced into the room. "Let's not panic. Everybody, walk out single file. No running or shoving. I'm sure there's nothing to worry about." He tried to sound reassuring.

"Nothing for him to worry about, anyway," Scott said.

"You don't know that it's Hezekiah Bones. It could be anything," I said as we moved out of our row and into the aisle.

"I repeated the story. Now I'll have to pay the price," Scott said gloomily. He shuffled behind me until we were just about to the door, then he stopped.

"What's wrong?" I asked.

"I left something under the seat. I've got to get it," he said. Before I could stop him, he was gone.

I glanced back just before I went out the double doors to the hallway. Scott was bending over and grabbing something under the seat. In another

15

minute he would be back in line with us all. I would have to meet him outside.

As we gathered around the flagpole on the front lawn of the school's campus, I looked around for Scott. But he hadn't come out. He had disappeared, or . . . ? Surely he wasn't invisible?

I was starting to worry.

Just then the teacher spoke to us. "Class, it was nothing to be alarmed about. We discovered that one of your classmates set off a stink bomb in the room. If any of you have an idea who did it, let me know. Or if you would like to confess to it, we will go easier on you."

I heard a muffled laugh behind me. I turned around, and with just one look, I knew the kid had done it. I think the teacher knew too because he was walking over to the boy.

The teacher touched him on the shoulder and said, "Mel, you wouldn't have had anything to do with that, would you?"

Mel smiled a big angelic smile and said, "Oh, not me, sir. I was on the other side of the room."

"What side was that, Mel?" the teacher asked.

"The left side," he answered.

"Hmm, that's the side we found it on."

"That's impossible. I thr—I mean, I thought I saw the kids on the other side smell it first." Mel tried to maneuver his way out of almost getting caught.

The teacher frowned at Mel and said, "Do you realize that if you got suspended, you wouldn't be able to play basketball?"

Mel bowed his head and said, "I didn't do it, but I know who did."

"Then maybe you can come with me," the teacher told Mel. As we all moved inside, Mel turned back to his friends and winked.

When we got back inside the auditorium, I looked around for Scott. He wasn't there. I asked a few of the others if they had seen him but no one had laid eyes on him since we had to evacuate the room.

Where could he have gone? Or maybe he hadn't gone anywhere. Maybe Scott was walking around the school in an invisible form.

No, that was impossible. The terrible smell had been a stink bomb, *not* Hezekiah Bones.

Scott must be somewhere.

As the day progressed, I asked different kids if they had seen him. No one had. It was as though he had disappeared off the face of the earth or at least off the campus of Crider Middle School.

Scott didn't show up in our last class, and the teacher was concerned. I wanted to stand up and say that Scott had been turned invisible by Hezekiah Bones. Instead, I sat there afraid that everyone would think I was too weird. I barely remember the rest of the class. My mind was on Scott and trying to find him. I hoped I would see Iza and Kris after school. I needed to tell them what happened.

The hallways were crowded with kids trying to get out of school. It took me a while to get through the leaping, laughing sea of students. By the time I reached my locker, Kris and Iza were waiting about five feet from the cursed locker that stood next to mine. With the side door open and kids escaping, the smell was not nearly so bad.

I called to them, "Did either of you see Scott this afternoon?"

Iza shrugged her shoulders and said, "No. His locker is next to mine, but he didn't show up after class. Is everything all right?"

"I'm not sure." The two of them could tell from my worried frown that something was wrong.

"What is it, Caitlin?" Kris said. She moved toward me.

"Do you remember that Scott told me that he would finish the story about the curse on Hezekiah's locker?"

They both nodded their heads yes, and I went on. "In study hall he went over the whole story after telling me that there is a curse on anyone who tells another person about it."

"That's right. If you tell someone then you get turned invisible for twenty-four hours," Iza said with surprise.

18

"Well, after he told me the whole story, somebody threw a stink bomb in the auditorium.

"The class got up to leave the room and go outside when Scott said that he forgot something under his seat and had to go back in. I was already heading out of the room and then outside. Scott never showed up on the front lawn."

"Wow, that means he could be invisible at this very minute and standing right next to us," Kris said.

Iza started looking around us. "Scott, hi, this is Isabella. We want to help you, but we can't see you. We need you to give us some kind of sign that you are here."

I felt like I was in a scene from some low-budget horror movie, but Iza kept talking until she suddenly stopped. Her mouth went open in surprise, and her eyes grew like full moons. I turned to see what had scared her.

From out of nowhere, a piece of notebook paper was floating toward us.

The floating paper dropped at my feet.

I was afraid to pick it up so I said, "Kris, it is addressed to you."

Kris hesitated before bending down. Without touching it she started to read it. "Dear Kris, I'm sorry that I have to cancel our after-school study time, but that big goof finally got me. You won't be seeing me until my time is up. Scott."

Iza put her hand to her mouth and asked, "What does it mean?"

"It means Scott was down by my locker and heard us. He must have walked the note down here, and he saw us. He felt so bad that he couldn't be around and he left the note on the floor," Kris said.

"Maybe he's still here," I told them. Then I started talking to our invisible friend. "Scott, I'm sorry that I had you tell me the story about the curse. Let me help you in some way. Can I talk to your mother?"

There was no answer. I turned around to the

haunted locker and spoke directly at it. "Hezekiah Bones, I believe in Jesus and I *don't* believe in you! Now, I want my friend turned visible again."

As soon as the words were out of my mouth I felt stupid. In the same breath, I'd said I didn't believe in curses and said to make Scott visible again.

In my frustration, I took one of the books in my hands and threw it at Hezekiah Bones's locker. It smacked the door, bounced back, and landed on my foot. Then the whole hall reverberated with a spooky o-o-o-o-ing sound.

The three of us jumped into the air just before we heard the laughter behind us. Mel and his friends were standing at the end of the hallway.

"I don't think our resident ghost would like being disrespected like that," Mel said as he moved toward us with his friends behind him.

"You need to be more careful, or the curse will get you," Mel continued. "Just your book touching it could already have done it."

"There's no such thing as a locker being cursed," I shot back in embarrassed anger. "That's just a superstition."

"If it is only a superstition, why don't you touch the locker and prove your point to everyone," Mel teased.

"I don't need to touch the locker to prove there is no curse. It's probably filled with somebody's old, stinky gym shoes," I retorted. "I don't think there was ever a Hezekiah Bones to begin with."

"You're afraid! How in the world are you going to make it on the basketball team if you're so afraid of a little curse?" he taunted.

I caught Kris with my eyes. "Don't tell me he's on the team?" I whispered to her.

"He's the star player," she whispered back.

I put my hands on my hips and stared right at him. "Curses and basketball have nothing to do with each other. I'm not afraid on the basketball court and I'm not afraid of this locker. Jesus *is* with me wherever I go."

"Jesus! What's Jesus got to do with it? You may have me and Jesus fooled, but you can't even convince yourself."

He was right. I couldn't even convince myself that I wasn't afraid or that I didn't believe in the curse. How could I let Jesus down this way? Maybe I was just all talk.

After seeing—or rather not seeing—Scott and then finding his note, I had begun to believe in the curse of Hezekiah Bones.

"I don't want to talk about this anymore. I need to get to the gym," I told the others, and took a step backward toward my locker. My foot stepped on an object lying on the floor and went out from under me.

I started to fall.

Without thinking, I jammed my right arm out behind me and caught myself on a locker handle.

I was embarrassed to look at everyone after being so clumsy. But when I raised my eyes, no one was smiling.

No one was laughing.

No one even grinned.

Mel and his friends, stunned and shocked, with eyes wide with fright, turned and bolted down the hall.

I looked at Kris and Iza. Their faces looked drained and stressed.

What had happened? Had I touched the cursed locker? I turned around to look.

My fingers were wrapped around the handle of Hezekiah Bones's locker.

And green ooze was working its way along my knuckles.

Grabbing a towel from my locker, I wiped frantically at the jellylike ooze, splashing some up my arm and down my leg before I could get it all off.

Kris and Iza, their eyes fixed on the green ooze, backed away.

"I've got to go. I'll meet you in the gym," Kris said.

"Please wait up, Kris. I promise not to touch you," I said. I was starting to believe that I had the curse.

"It was an accident, not a curse. I tripped over this book." I bent over and picked it up. I extended it for the other two to see.

Iza screamed, "No! it can't be!"

"What's wrong, Iza? What is it?" Kris asked as she grabbed her arm.

"That book is the one I gave to Scott this morning. It's the newest SpineChillers™. He must have dropped the book so Caitlin would trip over it. He must still be here," Iza told us with a shaky voice.

I looked around in what I hoped was his direction

and said, "Scott, why did you do that? Is it part of your curse? Talk to us, Scott."

There was no response.

I glanced at the other two who were sliding slowly away from me. "Come on now. This is all silly. Kris, let's go to the gym and play some basketball."

Kris nodded her head in agreement, but I noticed that the two of them kept lots of distance between them and me. By the time Kris and I reached the girls' locker room, the news of my recent misfortune had already spread to everyone.

The other girls were so afraid that I would touch them that they dressed in the shower stalls and avoided eye contact with me.

I knew I had to make a decision. Either my faith was going to beat this thing or I was going to be a scaredy-cat the rest of my life.

I got onto the court and did some stretches to loosen up my muscles. I was feeling very tight from all the tension of the last half hour.

The rest of the team was gathered under the one hoop at the other end of the court. They were taking turns shooting. Not one of them would come to my end of the court to shoot.

The coach entered and blew her whistle. Coach Fancher was a tall woman with stern eyes and a smiling face. At least it smiled for a little while.

Coach Fancher walked over next to me and turned

to the others. She said, "Crider Cats, we have a new player. Caitlin James comes from a school that had both boys' and girls' teams. She was the leading scorer in her division.

"This will be her first experience at coed ball, however, so let's play a little practice game.

"Red team and blue team on the court. Caitlin will play guard on the red team. Mel, you'll play opposite her."

Mel's face grew long. He would have to guard me but be sure not to touch me. It gave me an advantage and I used it. Every time I got the ball I drove to the basket, leaped, and did a layup. The red team was up by 16 when Coach Fancher stepped on the wooden floor and blew her whistle. My faith was starting to build.

"*Both* teams are to play offense and defense. Mel, I know that you're trying to be nice to Caitlin, but we need to see what she can do against a real defense. Let's double-team her this time," she finished and moved off the court.

As Coach Fancher's whistle blew, the two players guarding me did their best to stay away and at the same time stop me. I still scored several more points before practice ended.

I laughed inside and thought of Romans 8:28, "God works for the good of those who love him."

Coach Fancher walked me to the locker room

door as she said, "They really are much better than they played today. They should loosen up by tomorrow. We're glad that you're here. I've been looking for another strong female player."

"Thanks. I'm excited about playing here, but it has been a pretty crazy first day of school," I confessed.

"I must admit that Crider does seem to be unusual. After a while, the weirdness kind of grows on you. But no matter, we're both going to be part of the championship team," she said with a big smile.

Coach Fancher almost made me forget the rest of my terrible day. Her encouraging comments reminded me of my former youth choir director, who always knew what to say to calm my nerves when I got a case of stage fright before singing solo.

I headed into the rows of metal lockers and wooden benches. I was feeling better than I had all day. The coach thought I was a good player, and I didn't have a rash even after touching Hezekiah's locker.

Kris was already in the shower so I decided to just dress and shower at my house. That way Kris and Iza and I could all walk home together. I rounded the corner and headed to my locker.

Something strange was hanging from the handle.

My good mood vanished the closer I got. When I saw what it was, slivers of fear crisscrossed my body.

I shoved my fist into my mouth to keep from screaming.

A filthy, stinky sock with a hand-lettered message dangled from the handle:

> You are cursed.
> I'm coming for you.
>
> Hezekiah Bones

The other girls moved around me to see what it was. One of them gasped. Kris came running out of the shower, her hair soaking wet. I moved backward and sat down.

"What is it, Caitlin?" Kris asked.

"The sock," I mumbled.

"What sock?" she asked.

"On my locker," I said softly.

One of the other girls handed it to Kris. She read it and dropped it to the floor. "It's probably just a joke. I'll bet Mel had something to do with it. Forget about it and change your clothes. We'll get out of here and by tomorrow this will all be forgotten," encouraged Kris.

I looked down for the sock. It was missing. "Where's the sock?"

The other girls moved away. One of them must have picked up the sock and hidden it, or the mysterious Hezekiah Bones had taken it away. I asked again, "Where's the sock? If someone doesn't tell me where it is, I'll start touching each one of you, spreading my curse."

That was the wrong thing to say. All the girls except Kris gathered up their basketball gear and raced from the room. I looked at Kris and shrugged my shoulders.

"What do we do now?" Kris asked.

"I don't know. I just wish I could start my first day at Crider Middle School all over again." I plopped down on the bench and sank my head into my hands.

Kris looked at me with caring eyes and asked, "Are you ready to go home now?"

"No, I think I'll sit here for a few minutes. I need to collect my thoughts and try to understand what's happening to me. I'll see you tomorrow," I told her. I flashed a fake smile to make her believe that I was fine.

"All right, I'll see you later." Kris disappeared out of the locker room.

I sat there feeling sorry for myself. So much for

my faith! What was I going to do? Most of the kids wouldn't ever want to be friends with me. Not even the basketball team wanted to get near me. I sat for a few more minutes, then gathered my clothes for the walk home. Maybe my mom would have some suggestions on how to turn this "lemon into lemonade" as she always said.

I had just thrown my last piece of clothing into my gym bag and was ready to walk out.

Then I heard a strange sound. A howling deep inside the school's walls drifted through the pipes above my head.

Is someone trying to play a joke on me again? I looked around the room. Nothing was there.

I had to get out of the locker room fast. But before I could reach the door, it swung shut with a loud slam. *The wind?* When I pushed against the door, it resisted.

The door was locked! *How can I get out?*

The howling and moaning outside the door reminded me that Hezekiah Bones had me right where he wanted me. *Will I end up as green ooze escaping from his locker?*

I decided to face him eye to eye or, better yet, girl to ghoul. I pounded on the door.

"Hezekiah Bones, I'm in here and I'm ready for you. Come and get me. We'll see who is the best on the basketball court." I pounded harder.

Chains rattled on the other side of the door. I heard a key slip into the tumbler.

The door popped loose and started to ease its way open. I prepared myself for my first glimpse of Hezekiah Bones. I prayed I would live to tell about it.

The door opened all the way. The man standing there wasn't at all like I expected Hezekiah Bones to look. He was a short, stocky man with a big smile and wearing a green custodian staff uniform. The name Jinx was sewed onto his shirt.

"Sorry, little lady, I thought everyone was gone, or I wouldn't have locked the doors," he said with his pleasant grin.

"That's okay. I'm just glad it was you. I thought it was somebody else at first," I said with a breath of relief.

He looked at me and said, "Hey, you're the new girl who is going to help our team win the championship. I can't wait. We haven't been this close since . . ."

I knew what he wanted to say. "Since Hezekiah Bones was here?" I asked.

"He was the greatest."

"Were you here when he played?" I inquired.

"No, he was way before my time, but my dad used to tell the story of how he disappeared. His locker has been kept just as it was that day. It's never been opened since," he said with the excitement of a storyteller spinning yarns about his great and powerful ancestors.

"I know. I've got the locker next to his."

"You haven't touched it, have you?"

"It was an accident. I tripped over a book that my invisible friend dropped behind me and fell against it. Accidents don't count, do they?" I pleaded for some sort of hopeful answer.

He looked shocked. "A friend of yours told the story and was turned invisible, and you touched the locker? My, my, this is bad news."

"Is there anything I can do to get rid of the curse?" I was grasping for any possible hope.

"I don't know. In all my years working here no one has ever touched it. But I'll tell you what I'll do. If anyone knows an answer, my father will have it. I'll ask and let you know," he said. His big grin had returned.

"Thanks," I said. I picked up my gym bag and headed out.

Dinner was almost ready by the time I got home. I dropped my gym bag at the foot of the stairs. Usually, Mom would not have been pleased with my doing that. But since my room was still filled with boxes just like every other room, she excused it.

"Hi, hon. How was your first day at school?" Mom asked.

"Terrible. I've got the worst locker in the school. Nobody wants to go near me. Even my friends won't touch me. I'm being chased by a six-foot ghoul that lives in a locker filled with green ooze. I turned a friend invisible, and there's a curse on me," I said dispiritedly.

"Come on now, Caitlin. Things can't be that bad. The first day in any school can feel like that. Tell me what really happened," she said with a laugh.

"That was what really happened," I insisted.

"How about basketball practice? Do you think you'll fit in there?" she said in an attempt to change the subject to something a little brighter.

"The team won't get near me," I said.

"Maybe they just need to get to know your style of playing."

"No, Mom, they won't come near me. They think that I've got a curse on me." I was trying to let her know how tough the day had been, but I wasn't very good at explaining.

"You are serious, aren't you, honey?" Mom's eyes grew concerned.

"Yes. It has been a really strange day. What do you know about curses?" I asked.

"I know that the Bible says God will never leave you or forsake you. But if it will make you feel better, why don't you call Ben? He can get some information about curses from the library," she said.

I was embarrassed to telephone my big brother with a problem, but I was getting desperate. I needed help!

When he came on the line, I was relieved I got him instead of his answering machine. "Hi, Ben. It's Caitlin. Mom thinks you can help me with a problem."

"Anytime, Sis. You know that," he said.

"I've got some really important stuff that I need to talk to someone about right away," I said.

"I've got an idea. Are you going to the school carnival tomorrow night?" he wanted to know.

"I hadn't decided, but I guess I could go."

"I'll tell you what we can do. I'll meet you at the carnival. When it's over, I can drive you home, and that'll give us some time to talk. How about it?"

"Great. I'll see you then." I hung up the phone and went back to the kitchen to see my mom, but she had gone to another room.

I grabbed my gym bag and tramped up the stairs to my room. I pushed a few boxes out of the way and threw myself on the bed.

I closed my eyes and drew in a long breath through my nose. That was when I got my first sniff of it. My room was filled with an unexplainable stench.

Hezekiah Bones was in my room!

"Ahh!" I yelled as I leaped into the air. My body slammed against a stack of boxes and sent them tumbling across the floor. The contents of the boxes became obstacles between me and the door.

I tried to leap a stack of books that were ready to go into my bookshelves, but I missed. My left foot sent the entire set of books teetering into another tower of cardboard boxes.

Like dominoes, the boxes bumped the desk chair, which in turn tipped over the tower of sports trophies.

Books and boxes and trophies littered my way. I couldn't get out. But then Hezekiah Bones probably couldn't get to me, either.

As I pushed boxes out of the way, the odor seemed to grow stronger. I finally got to the door but slipped on a magazine. The slick cover sent me plummeting once more to my bedroom floor.

I tried to pull myself up from the ruins of my room.

Suddenly, a hand gripped my arm. *Hezekiah had caught me.*

"Dinner is ready," Mom said as she pulled me to my feet. She looked around the room. "What happened up here?"

"Mom, what is that terrible smell in my room?" I asked in a near panic.

"We had some leakage in the plumbing behind your wall. The plumber opened it up to fix the problem, but now he wants to let the drywall material air out and dry before he patches the hole. The stench of a wet, musty inside wall is terrible, but the smell ought to be gone by tomorrow," Mom said.

She steadied me on my feet and then headed back down the hallway.

I straightened my clothes and followed her downstairs. Dad had a meeting with some new clients and wouldn't be in until late. Dinner was quiet. I didn't want to talk much. I had a lot on my mind.

After dinner, I worked hard to put away the items that were covering my floor. By bedtime, I was glad to shower and crawl into my cozy bed. As I lay there, I remembered that I used to pull the covers over my head when I was little. I used to think that a monster was trying to capture me.

Silly. But the next thing I knew I was pulling the covers over my head and praying.

Jesus? I know Mom's right and that you'll never

leave me or forsake me. I don't know why I'm letting this curse business get to me like this. I'll try to trust you better. And thanks for helping me play a good game today. 'Night, Jesus.

Before I ever wanted it, morning had come, and I was off to school. I thought it strange that no one in our house was up yet. I grabbed my gym bag and hit the streets. The sky was still tinged with gray by the time I reached the front door of the school.

I thought I was either late or early because nobody else was on the campus. I looked down to see the time, but my watch wasn't on my arm. With Hezekiah Bones on my mind I was forgetting everything else.

I climbed the stairs to the front door and pushed on it. It felt really heavy as I moved it inward and slipped inside the school.

The halls were empty. Could everyone be in the auditorium for an assembly? I moved toward the auditorium down a long hall.

The hall went on and on. I was sure it was going to go past my locker and then to where the other students were, but it just continued. The farther I went, the darker it got. Until finally I was moving along and guiding myself by the vibrations of my echoing feet. I couldn't believe that my custodian friend hadn't fixed the lights. A dark hallway could be dangerous. Hezekiah Bones could grab me and no one would know.

I had no more than thought about Hezekiah Bones when I heard footsteps behind me. I quickened my pace. So did the other steps. I tried to walk softly so the person following me would stop. It didn't work. The person walked softer.

I turned in hopes of seeing something. The hallway was dark. It was too dangerous to run. I would have to outsmart my shadow. I felt along the wall for a doorway or another hall. I moved slowly.

It had to be Hezekiah. His odor permeated the hall behind me.

Suddenly, my hand touched a door. But before I could open it, his large strong hand gripped my shoulder and turned me around.

I was only six inches away from Hezekiah's large, ugly face. "You were warned not to disturb my locker. But you did it anyway. Now you will pay . . ."

10

"No, no, let me go! I don't want to go into your locker. I don't want your lousy curse," I yelled.

"Caitlin! Caitlin!"

"Leave me alone!"

"Caitlin!"

"I don't want to get turned into green ooze," I shouted.

"Caitlin, wake up!"

My eyes popped open. Mom stood over me, shaking me by the arm. "Wake up, honey. It's time to get up for school. You must have been having a terrible nightmare. What were you dreaming about?"

"Nothing. I'm fine now," I told her.

"It must have been something because of the way you were screaming. What was all that about lockers and green ooze?" Mom inquired.

"Just a nightmare. The first day at school must have been tougher than I thought. It will be better today, I'm sure," I told her as I rolled over and looked at the clock. "Wow, I better get up and get out of here. Mom, remember that I'm going to the school carnival after practice tonight. Ben is going to bring me home afterward."

"Okay, honey. Now, get up and we'll have breakfast before you leave," she said. The way she smiled at me always made me feel better.

I got to school right on time, but the news of my curse got there ahead of me. The kids gave me a wide pathway to walk. I heard soft whispers of "Hezekiah Bones" with each step I took.

When I turned the bend by my locker, I saw Mel and his friends standing by it. Hanging on the handle was the sock from the night before.

"Real funny, Mel. Now that you've had your little joke on me maybe I can get into my locker and start classes," I told him as I walked toward my locker.

At first none of them moved out of the way. I extended an arm, and the two girls nearest me backed away. I continued toward the locker when Mel stepped in front of me.

"Listen, Caitlin. I just want you to know that if Hezekiah Bones grabs you and drags you into the locker and turns you into green ooze, then I'll start a fund drive to raise money for a niče burial marker to be placed over Hezekiah's locker," he said. He started to laugh. The rest of the kids laughed along with him. The morning had not started out well at all.

Mel's friends moved out of the hallway, and I yanked the sock from the handle and pulled open the door to the locker. I half expected something to jump out at me, but nothing did. So far that seemed to be the only thing that had gone my way all morning.

In my first class, every empty seat seemed to be "saved" for someone else. It wasn't until the teacher walked into the room that the desks became available. I looked around for Scott. He was supposed to be in the class. I didn't see him, but then again if he was invisible, I wouldn't see him anyway.

As the teacher started the lesson, I saw a girl hand a note to a boy one row over from me. He read it and looked at me. Then he folded it and passed it to the boy behind him.

The piece of notebook paper made it halfway around the class before the teacher spied a girl passing it.

The teacher grabbed it from her and opened it up. She looked at me and then folded it again, tossing the note into the wastebasket.

"Caitlin, you shouldn't pay attention to all this silliness about Hezekiah Bones and a curse. It is all nonsense and superstition."

I smiled. I wanted to believe what she said, but my nightmare had really shaken me up. My faith wasn't getting stronger—it was losing ground. I knew what Mom told me was true, but so far everything indicated that the curse was real. Except for one thing. I hadn't broken out in a rash.

When the bell rang, I headed to the next class. Iza met me by the door. "It's all over the school. I tried to stop the rumor, but it was hopeless."

"That's okay, Iza. I can handle it," I told her as I scratched my left arm. "It will all blow over as soon as people realize that there is no truth to the story."

I went into the room and slid into a desk before anyone could make any excuses. I put my books under the seat and grabbed my pencil. Before I started writing, I used it to scratch my back.

About halfway through the class, I noticed that I had been scratching my left arm and left leg.

A few minutes later I was scratching harder and harder.

I was afraid to look. If the curse wasn't true, then it was impossible for me to have the rash. Wasn't it?

My left arm was bright beet red and disgustingly bumpy. The curse of Hezekiah Bones was true. I didn't know what to do.

The rash drove me crazy. I wanted to scratch it, but the others would notice what was happening. I bit my lip to keep from scratching. My nails were extended and ready to pull across my red rashy flesh.

I didn't think I could keep from scratching for another minute. I could think of only one thing to do: sit on my hands to keep myself from looking like a chimpanzee in the zoo. I was no longer concentrating on the teacher's instructions.

That was a mistake.

"Caitlin, have you already covered this material in your other school?"

"What?" I responded.

"Have you already covered this material? Perhaps that's why you aren't listening," the teacher said. I really like science, but she was right, I wasn't listening.

"I'm sorry, but I'm not feeling well. Could I have

a hall pass? I need to see the nurse," I told her. It was the first thing that came into my mind, but everybody in the school was going to know that I had to go to the nurse.

As she wrote the hall pass, I could see a new note making its way around the class. By the time I got to the nurse's office, the whole school would know that Caitlin James had a rash from the Hezekiah Bones curse.

The itch was driving me mad. It was going to be a long walk.

The urge to scratch was unbearable, but I managed to walk down the first corridor without ripping the skin off my arm.

It wasn't a normal rash. How could the nurse possibly help?

As I tried to think, I kept moving down the hall. I heard a noise. I turned around but didn't see anything. Just like in my dream.

I started to hurry, but there it was again. I heard the soft padding of feet behind me. I turned. No one was there.

I walked at a quicker pace. I heard the steps again. Closer. They were a lot closer. Then they stopped. I turned, but no one was there. It had to be my imagination. Because of the dream, my mind was making up those footsteps behind me. Sure. That was it. Just my imagination.

I started my forward progress down the hall again.

After a few seconds the steps behind me started again. I tried to smile. I wasn't going to let my imagination get to me. I said a silent prayer and kept walking. My smile spread wide across my face.

As I turned the corner, I felt it.

A hand gripped my shoulder. My nightmare was no longer a dream. Hezekiah's real hand stopped me in my tracks.

"What are you doing out here, young lady?"

I spun around and looked at Miss Wiley, the vice principal.

What a relief!

"I don't know what you are so happy about. Where is your hall pass?"

I stretched out my arm in front of her and extended my hall pass. "I'm going to the nurse's office to have her look at this rash," I told her.

"I'll walk you there. That's my job. I make sure that you kids are not out causing trouble. I make sure that you kids act properly," she retorted.

"Is that what you were doing when you followed me through the halls?" I inquired.

"What kind of question is that? I was looking into the classrooms to observe any misbehavior that might be occurring," she stated in her stern, raspy voice.

"That explains it," I told myself, but she heard me say it out loud.

"Explains what?" Miss Wiley quizzed. Her questions made me feel as if I had a bright light shining in my face.

"I kept looking back to see who was following me but never saw anyone. I must have turned around while you were looking in the door windows. You would have been blocked from my sight by the lockers," I said.

I had reached the nurse's office. "Nice to meet you," I told her as I moved away from her.

When I pushed open the door to the nurse's office, the antiseptic aroma hit me. A white uniform was wrapped around a twig of a woman who wore an old-fashioned nurse's hat.

"Hello, dear. Can I help you?" she said with a beaming white smile.

"Yes. I have this rash on my arm. It itches terribly, and I think that it's spreading."

"Come and sit down. Let me have a look at it, dear," she said in her pleasant voice. I rolled up my sleeve and showed her my inner left arm. She looked closely at it and then sat back in her chair.

"Can you tell me what it is?" I asked, hoping that it was something simple like an allergy to chalk dust.

"Have you been near the locker that smells grossly awful?" she asked seriously.

"Yes. Mine is right next to it."

"Have you touched it in any way?"

48

"Yesterday I tripped over a book and reached out to keep myself from falling and accidentally touched it. I don't think that curses get transferred by accidental contact," I said. I hoped that she would agree with me.

"Who said anything about a curse?" the nurse asked.

"You know, the curse of Hezekiah Bones," I told her with surprise.

"That old fairy tale. I hope that the other kids don't have you believing in the curse of Hezekiah Bones," she said as if she were dismissing a kid from a class.

"Then why did you ask about his locker?"

"I have my suspicions about the green ooze that seeps out of it," the nurse told me.

"Is there anything I can take or put on it to stop the itching?" I had to find something to stop my wild desire to scratch.

The nurse pulled a tube of ointment from a drawer and told me to rub it on every hour. Then she sent me to my next class.

Through each class, I noticed the itching started to lessen but each time I rolled up my sleeve to apply the ointment, all the others stared at me. By lunchtime, kids were staying 10 feet away from me in the cafeteria.

Iza and Kris strolled through the cafeteria doors

moments after I sat down at a long, empty table. I had started to feel really sorry for myself as they approached me.

"How's it going today, Caitlin?" Kris inquired.

"About the same as yesterday, but now everyone knows that I have the curse. There's a new twist to it," I told them. I rolled up my sleeve, and the red bumpy rash glowed in their faces.

"Wow, not good. Not good at all, Caitlin," Iza said softly.

I knew that the two girls cared, but they had known me only twenty-four hours. Why would they risk their social lives to be friends with me?

Kris tried to change the subject. "Has anyone seen Scott yet?"

Iza and I shook our heads from side to side. He wasn't at school, or at least we couldn't see him if he was.

"Should we report it to the principal's office?" I asked.

"Report what?" Kris scoffed. "That our friend Scott has turned invisible because of the curse of Hezekiah Bones? 'By the way, Dr. Wiser, our friend Caitlin is cursed as well, and she should be quarantined.' I don't think so. Let's keep it to ourselves until we have more proof."

The three of us ate lunch in silence. No one knew what to say or do. When the bell rang, I sucked in a breath and waited for most of the kids to clear the cafeteria.

The next class was about the same as the preceding ones. Notes were passed. Whispers floated in the air. Quick glances and long, intense stares came my way. I was getting used to it, but I had still decided to ask my mother to home school me. Life would be a lot easier.

I knew what Mom would say. "Caitlin, we do not run from our problems. With Jesus' help, we face them and we learn from them." That was easy to say for someone without a curse.

I had study hall following that class. With Scott still invisible, I would have no one to sit near. I thought, *Scott may be there in his invisible state, and if he is, maybe he'll know what to do next.*

I started to scurry down the hall. I wanted to get to the seat next to his before someone else grabbed it. I was moving so quickly that kids had to leap out of my way to avoid touching me. I headed through the doorway to the auditorium and looked at Scott's seat. I couldn't believe it. He was sitting there as visible as anyone else in that class.

He hadn't seen me yet. I was ready to race up the aisle when the teacher in charge called my name. "Ms. James." I tried to ignore him, but he got louder. "Ms. James, could I have a word with you?"

I turned to the man who taught history and looked at him. "What did I do?" I wondered out loud.

"Nothing, nothing at all. The school office sent this over for you to read. It's information about the school," he said.

I thanked him and turned around to talk to Scott. He was gone.

I hurried to the row. Scott's backpack and books were there. Was he invisible again? At least I knew where he was and could talk to him.

I slipped into the seat next to his. "Hi, Scott. I know you're there. You became visible for a second or two. It must be wearing off," I whispered at ear level. I wished he could respond.

"The curse has hit me full force. I discovered the rash a few classes before this one. The whole school already knows about it. How can I get rid of the curse?"

No response.

"Try to remember everything that you've seen or heard so you can tell us later what it was like to be invisible."

I did want to know what it would be like to be invisible. I slouched down in the auditorium seat and tried to imagine what I would do if I was invisible. Maybe as a joke I could lower the basketball hoop by about two feet so I could slam-dunk when I was visible. Or maybe I could sit with the teachers and find out what they talk about when students aren't around.

I continued to imagine what it would be like until I felt a sharp jab in my ribs. "Hey, you dozed off."

My eyes snapped open. It was Scott's voice, and I was hoping that I would see him in flesh and blood. Sure enough, he was sitting beside me—clearly visible.

"Scott!" I said loudly.

Everybody looked our way. Scott was a very quick thinker, and he grabbed a tissue and pretended to sneeze. The kids laughed, and the teacher went back to correcting his papers.

I whispered out of the side of my mouth, "Pretty smooth."

"Thanks," he said. Then he continued, "I need to tell you what happened."

"Iza, Kris, and I already know. We have so many questions for you about the experience," I said quietly.

"Sure, I'll tell you all at the carnival tonight," he whispered back just as the teacher looked up. Scott and I dropped our heads and pretended to read. I tore a sheet of paper out of my notebook and wrote a big *OK* on it. He smiled, and we went back to quietly waiting.

All my questions burst out when the bell rang. "So,

what was it like? Where did you stay? What did your parents say? Did you find out anything about the curse?"

"Hold it, Caitlin. Let me try to explain. At first, I didn't think it was anything unusual happening to me. But it continued to spread around my body," Scott said. "I've got to go now, but I'll tell you all more when we get to the carnival." He darted down the hall to his next class.

I think I would have been a lot more animated had I been invisible for the last 24 hours.

Classes went a little smoother after study hall. I think most of the kids had already talked about me enough. I was getting to be old news to everyone except Hezekiah Bones. I knew I had to be number one on his hit list.

I slipped through the halls quickly after school and went to the locker room. I got there before the others arrived. I pulled a heavy gray sweat suit over my basketball workout clothes. I wanted to practice my layups, and I didn't want anyone to see how far and how fast the rash was spreading.

Practice seemed better. No one got near enough to touch me, but at least I got a workout. I found out that Mel was good at basketball, and it was fun to play on the same team.

We banged the boards for an hour. The coach called it quits so we could all make it to the carnival on time. She also wanted to give us a small pep talk because of the big game coming up.

"As you all know, Upper Darby Middle School is probably the only other team in our division that could beat us for the championship. We have only one opportunity to play them during the season. The outcome of this game on Tuesday night will predict this year's championship team," Coach Fancher cautioned.

"How often have we beaten them?" I asked innocently.

"Well, Caitlin, Upper Darby has a winning streak going against us," she answered.

"How many games in a row?" I asked. The groans that came from around me and the pained look on the coach's face told me there were a lot.

"We started losing to them on the night that . . ." Coach Fancher stopped in the middle of the sentence.

"On the night that what?" I urged.

Mel moved up behind me and said, "On the night that Hezekiah Bones disappeared. They have been beating us every year since then."

Another team player spoke up next. "Yes, and the school board is getting ready to shut down Crider Middle School and ship us all to Upper Darby. If we can win the championship, we can stay here."

"I didn't realize that so much was riding on this game," I told them all.

"I didn't want to put any pressure on you," the coach apologized.

We all headed back to the locker rooms in a quiet hush. It was an important game coming up. I needed to work on my game a little harder. I wondered what would happen if I was invisible or covered with a rash from head to toe. I wouldn't be much help to the team that way. I needed to find the cure for my curse.

As I was walking into the locker room, the coach spoke to me. She needed me to fill her in on my playing record. It didn't take that long, but by the time I got down to the locker room, the other girls were gone. I was hoping that it would not be a repeat of the night before when I got scared by the school custodian.

While I was showering, the thought came to me that maybe Mr. Jinx had found out from his father how to cure the curse. I hurried through drying off and pulled my clothes back on. I had to get out of the locker room and find him.

I finished tying my shoes, and I was ready to bolt out the door. A deep, resonating pounding sound stopped me. *It must be Mr. Jinx*, I thought. The sound moved along the wall until it reached the door. I smiled and pushed the door open.

"Surprise!" I yelled in my attempt to scare him, but no one was there. I stepped into the workout room across the hall and flipped on the light switch. No one in that room, either.

I turned to leave when I heard the door at the end of the hall swing closed.

The only other sound was my heavy breathing.

I listened and then called out, "Who's there?" I saw someone do that in a movie. I thought it was dumb when he did it, and it was probably pretty dumb when I did it.

If Hezekiah Bones was there, he wouldn't announce that he was coming to get me.

I waited another minute and moved to the dark hallway. I was about to make a quick dash for the door when I heard it creak open.

I leaped back into the workout room. I glanced around, hoping to find something to use as a weapon. I saw only exercise machines. And I didn't think I could manage to protect myself with one of them.

The heavy metal door swung shut again with a tremendous bang. Footsteps moved down the hallway toward me.

I remembered that Dad always told me that the best defense was a good offense. So I leaped into the hallway and shouted, "Aha!"

My screaming, leaping body scared the hallway monster. He stopped and put his hand to his chest and said, "Wow, that was quite a scare, Caitlin. I guess you owed me one."

The custodian! "I'm so sorry, Mr. Jinx. I thought you were . . ."

"Hezekiah Bones?" he interrupted.

"Yes, but you're not. Hezekiah Bones is much taller," I said with a smile.

He smiled back and said, "And much, much thinner."

"Did your father know how to get rid of the curse?" I got right to the subject that was getting under my skin.

"That was what I was coming to tell you. I had hoped I wouldn't miss you," he told me. "My dad wasn't very talkative. The only thing he said was, 'It is the end next Tuesday.' I asked him whose end, Caitlin's or Hezekiah's? He answered, 'Either.'"

I gulped to get some wetness in my mouth so I could tell him thanks anyway. I croaked it out and then asked, "Can you tell me more of the story of Hezekiah Bones?"

"I don't know much more than what I said yesterday. Hezekiah went to school here a long time ago. His family had always been very tall. All the tall sons married tall women, and all the tall daughters married tall men. The whole clan kept getting taller and taller.

"Hezekiah developed early, much like you. Because of his height, the Crider basketball team won every game for three years. It was his last one. It was the championship game against the town rival, Upper Darby.

"Upper Darby had kept the score close, but Hezekiah stood between them and winning. Hezekiah broke a shoestring and left the court to get a new one. That was the last time anyone ever saw him."

"Why is his locker still there?" I asked.

"The school kept it that first year in case he returned. By the time that the next year's first day of school rolled around, it was fused shut. No one could get it open. It's been left like that ever since."

Mr. Jinx swallowed and nodded his head to indicate the validity of the story.

"Do you believe it?" I asked.

"Sometimes, when I'm in the school all by myself, I hear noises. Is it just my imagination that I hear the basketball bounce in the gym but no one's there? That I hear footsteps behind me in the hall but no one's there?

"When I sweep the floor by your locker, is it my imagination that I hear the moans of Hezekiah's past victims?

"But the scariest thing is when I'm down here and those big metal doors start to shake. What if Hezekiah is trying to find that shoestring?" he ended.

All of a sudden, the big metal door at the end of the hall started to shake violently.

We heard the sound of the handle turning and the first creak of the door opening.

Mr. Jinx's eyes were wide with terror as he stared past me at the door.

15

I pulled in a big breath just before letting out a blood-curdling scream.

The door swung open. In the light of the stairway stood three silhouettes: Scott, Iza, and Kris.

"Hurry, Caitlin, the carnival is starting," Kris called.

Whew! I hastily waved good-bye to Mr. Jinx and ran out the door. I followed my friends to the hall by my locker.

I stopped them and asked, "Can you wait while I throw my bag in here and get some things?" I dropped the gym bag inside and grabbed a big floppy hat and some sunglasses.

Iza screwed up her eyebrows and asked, "What are those for?"

"I was hoping that a disguise would allow me to move freely around the carnival without causing people to stampede in the other direction," I told them as we strolled through the hall, laughing at my plan.

Every year Crider Middle School held the carnival a few days before the big game with Upper Darby. Lots of rides were brought in on semitrailers. Bright colored lights illuminated the field behind the school, and kids ran excitedly between the merry-go-round and the little cars that circled endlessly.

I've always loved carnivals. But the way my life was going, this could end up being my carnival of terror.

The four of us walked through the midway. I wanted Scott to tell us what it was like being invisible, but the music booming from each ride was so loud that we couldn't hear very well.

Scott stopped in front of the Haunted House of Horror. It was not much bigger than two semitrailers. I declined right away. "I've had enough of ghosts and ghouls and haunted things that get stuffed into lockers. I'll wait out here."

Iza pleaded with me. "Come on, Caitlin. You could take off your disguise inside and be like everyone else."

"I am like everyone else," I retorted.

"I didn't mean it like that. I'm sorry. I just meant that you wouldn't have to wear the disguise," she apologized.

I still shook my head no.

"What's the matter? Are you scared?" Scott asked.

"No, I'm not scared. I touched the locker, didn't I? I'm not afraid of Hezekiah or haunted houses." I folded my arms over my chest as I said it and dug my heels into the ground.

I frowned and gritted my teeth but finally said, "Let's go. It can't be any worse than what I'm already going through." We climbed the steps to the entrance. I pulled off my sunglasses and walked in.

The first tiny room was filled with plastic spiders and cheap sound effects. Scott turned to me and said, "If this is too scary for you, we can leave."

I started laughing and told him, "I think I can handle it." I kept laughing until we passed into the second room. In that room I nearly fell over from laughter. All of us were roaring.

Across from us was what must have been the world's cheapest-looking mannequin dressed like Dracula. A motor had been attached to one arm, making the arm look as if it motioned for us to come forward. A taped voice was saying, "Come into my Haunted House of Horror." They needed a new tape. The one playing was garbled, and it went fast and then slow. We laughed harder.

The four of us laughed our way into the next section. The door shut behind us, leaving us in total darkness.

Kris was first in our line inside the narrow hall. I stayed dead last so I wouldn't touch anyone by accident. Even my friends wanted to keep a safe distance from me.

"Kris, you'll have to lead us through here," Iza said.

As we moved forward, we put out our hands to feel our way along the hall. The walls felt as if they were covered with bugs and things.

"This stuff is nothing but rubber. Go ahead and grab something, and you'll see what I mean," Scott instructed.

I heard Iza and Kris laugh as they touched the wall and discovered fake scary things. I didn't have the same luck. I grabbed what felt like a hand, and it began to move, then it gripped me back. I yelled, "A hand has grabbed me. Help me!"

Iza said, "Hold on, I'm coming."

Scott stopped her. "Watch out, Iza. You'll catch Hezekiah's curse."

"Someone, help!" I yelped.

"No need to," Kris announced. "You grabbed my hand. Sorry to scare you."

What a relief. We moved from the dark hall into a room filled with mirrors that made us look weird.

I found a tall, thin mirror that was stuck far back in one corner. It made me look even taller. I was snickering to myself when some boy that I didn't know moved behind me to look in the mirror next.

He looked tall, thin, and . . . horrifying.

Terror rooted me to the spot.

Only one person looked like that.

16

As soon as I could move I went tearing by my friends and out the exit. I hit the exit door hard and smashed it open. I leaped to the grass below and fell. My hat flew off and my sunglasses popped out of my blouse pocket.

I heard a few kids say, "It's the girl with the curse" before I could gather my disguise and put it back on.

While I was dusting myself off, the other three came flying out of the Haunted House behind me. I turned around to look at them and a hand gripped my shoulder. I screamed and pulled away.

"Wow, that must be some haunted house if all of you are so jumpy." It was Ben. I gave him a big smile and a sigh of relief as I looked up at his red hair and freckled face.

"How is it going so far?" he asked us.

"We're having fun, I think," Iza answered.

"Caitlin, how about if you meet me back here in an hour?" Ben wanted to know.

"Sure, that will give me a whole hour to get more frightened," I told him.

"Good, I'm glad to see that you'll use that time constructively," he joked. "Remember, between the Haunted House and the merry-go-round in an hour." He waved good-bye to us as he walked down the midway.

The four of us tried to decide what to do next. "What about that thing that goes around and around while it tilts on its side?" Iza asked.

Kris and Scott thought it was a great idea, but I decided to sit the ride out. If I had only an hour left, I wanted to see some of the other amusements. I headed toward the booths, games, and sideshows.

The barkers for the sideshows were trying to get people in, but I ignored them until I got to "Fantastic Fred's Feats of the Mind." Fantastic Fred had just hypnotized a man and made him sing "Happy Birthday" and eat imaginary cake.

He was about to bring the man out of the trance when he looked at the audience and said, "Who else? Do I have another volunteer?"

No one raised a hand or made a sound.

Fantastic Fred snapped his fingers, and the man came out of the trance, insisting that he could not be hypnotized. The people were laughing until Fantastic Fred called again for a volunteer.

No sound came from the audience.

He looked right at me "Young lady in the floppy hat and sunglasses, let me hypnotize you. Step right up here."

"No thanks, I've had enough excitement for one day."

I continued to decline his proposal as I backed away—and bumped into somebody.

Turning around, I opened my mouth to apologize.

It was the same tall, thin, horrifying person who'd sent me running from the hall of mirrors in the Haunted House of Horror.

A scream came out instead.

17

I raced back toward the midway to find my friends. I turned the corner of a large, red-striped tent and smacked right into them.

Iza went flying backward while Kris and Scott grabbed my sweatshirt to stop my body from continuing to the ground. Unfortunately, Iza had no one to stop her fall. I walked over to her and extended my hand to help her up.

Iza laughed and said, "Well, we were just wondering where you were. I told the others that we would probably run into you soon. I guess I was right. Although I didn't mean it literally."

"I'm sorry, but I was down by the sideshows and Fantastic Fred wanted to hypnotize me. I said no and backed into somebody. I turned around. I'm sure it was Hezekiah Bones. He's the one who scared us at the Haunted House. He must have been following me," I explained without taking a breath.

"Let's see if we can find him. I want to see what Hezekiah Bones looks like," Kris said.

We searched the carnival. We even went on the Ferris wheel in hopes that we could see him from such a high spot. No luck. He was nowhere to be found.

We had to give up our search when it was time for me to meet Ben. We walked to his car from the merry-go-round. I said good-bye to my three friends who were going to stay a little longer.

I climbed into the front seat and took off my hat and sunglasses. Without waiting for an invitation to talk I blurted out, "I have the curse of Hezekiah Bones."

"I've heard some kind of made-up mumbo jumbo about a cursed locker in your school," Ben said. "Apparently the locker stinks and hasn't been opened since some guy named Hezekiah Bones disappeared in the middle of a basketball game. Crider has not been able to beat Upper Darby since that day, and any kid who touches the locker gets the curse."

Ben looked at me. "I take it that you touched the locker?"

"It's right next to mine, and I tripped and fell against it by accident. I didn't think that you could get the curse if you touched something by accident," I told him.

"I haven't looked in the *Curse Rule Book* lately. I'll check that out," Ben joked. But he immediately became serious and said, "Tell me the rest of the story."

I told him about Scott turning invisible and the

green ooze and finally the rash on my body. I tried to describe all the weird happenings from the last two days in such a way that he would know how serious my problem was.

When I finished my story, I sat back.

"I'll look up some material on curses and fill you in on the subject as soon as I can. But for now, I'll tell you everything that I know," he said.

I prepared myself to hear about the horrible things that happen to people who get curses.

"As long as you love God and serve him, curses don't have any power over you. Remember 1 John 4:4? 'God's Spirit, who is in you, is greater than the devil, who is in the world.'

"On the other hand, people who are afraid of curses usually make them come true. Things happen because people expect them to happen."

"I don't understand," I told him.

"You are making the curse come true by yourself. It's called a self-fulfilling prophecy. You think it will happen so it does."

"I'm making up my own curse?" I asked.

"Kind of," he replied.

"Then why did Scott disappear? And why are terrible things happening to me? And what about this rash all over my body?" I asked.

"Caitlin, there's got to be an explanation for all this."

"Yes. Hezekiah Bones is going to drag me into his locker as my tomb."

We pulled up in front of the house. Ben turned to me. "Chin up, Caitlin. What reasons could there be for what is happening?"

I tried to smile a sincere thank-you when I got out of the car. He was trying to help, but he just didn't understand.

As I got to the porch, a horrible stench reached my nose. Had Hezekiah followed me home?

I yanked the front door open and bolted inside.

The smell was worse inside.

Why was Hezekiah here? Was he going to get my family too?

Pansy, my dog, was whimpering. The sound was coming from the kitchen. The poor thing must be in pain. What had Hezekiah done to her?

I moved carefully toward the kitchen. The keeper of the curse might be waiting there for me.

Just then my mother groaned. I was frightened, but I had to help her. I dashed into the kitchen.

As I flew through the door, Mom yelled again.

But instead of coming face-to-face with Hezekiah Bones, I smacked into Mom. She was standing at the sink holding Pansy down with one hand and with the other she was scrubbing her clean.

Mom looked at me and laughed.

"Honey, can you help me? Pansy got sprayed by a skunk. She was a little too curious.

"Hand me some more tomato juice. The smell is a lot better than it was."

"Phew. I don't even want to know what it smelled like before." I held my nose.

"How was school? and practice? Did you have fun at the carnival? Did you have a good talk with Ben?"

"The kids still don't want to come near me. At practice they had to get closer to guard me, but I still scored. I got scared a couple of times at the carnival, but I was able to handle it."

Mom assumed I meant that the rides were scary. I didn't want to worry her by telling her that Hezekiah Bones had been following me around the carnival.

"What about your ride home with Ben?" Mom wanted to know.

"Ben doesn't believe in curses. He thinks that when people expect something to happen that it usually does."

"Like a *self-fulfilling prophecy*?" she asked.

"That was exactly what he called it. I don't see how I'm causing anything to happen, though. How could I give myself a rash?

"I don't know what to think right now. Maybe it will all just go away," I said.

We kissed each other on the cheek and I went upstairs to my musty-smelling bedroom.

The next day at school went much like the day before. Kids were still afraid to go near me, but no one was talking about me. In fact, a few even said hello to me. That was progress as far as I was concerned.

History class had an unusual start. The teacher,

who is always there taking attendance, was missing. We all took the time to chat. Iza was in the class with me, and we talked about the carnival. She wanted to know what Ben had said.

Suddenly, the door to the room was yanked open, and a substitute teacher walked into the room. The man was tall and thin and looked like an aging version of the boy I ran into at the carnival.

He walked to the desk without saying a word. Several of the students around me turned and whispered, "We've got Hezekiah Bones as a teacher, and it's all your fault."

I wanted to yell at him, "Take me and leave all these innocent people alone," but that would have been too melodramatic.

The substitute teacher picked up chalk and moved to the board to write his name. First he put down the Mr. part. Then he started on his last name. It began with a *B*. I sucked in a fearful breath. The situation was not looking good for me.

The next letter was an *O*. Every eye in the room shot me an angry glance.

I dropped my head because I didn't want to see what he wrote next, but when I heard the gasp of the other students, I knew it was an *N*. Some of the others were gripping their books to their chests as if to protect themselves. I wanted to tell them to relax because he was there for me, not them.

His chalk scratched out the letter *E*.
We sucked in our breath. We waited fearfully for
him to finish writing the dreaded name.

The class broke into a howl of laughter. He had written a *T*, not an *S*. The French name *Bonet*!

"Good morning class, I am your substitute teacher today. My name is pronounced bo-nay. My family is new in town. My sister and her son and I have moved here. That is, I've moved here. They won't officially be here for another few days. My nephew will attend Crider Middle School," he told us.

Now I knew that Hezekiah Bones was coming to get me.

At the end of the day, Iza and Kris met me at my locker. They had something else on their minds.

"Have you seen the posters around the school about the talent show?" Kris asked.

"I did," I answered.

"Do you want to be in it?" she continued.

"I'd like to, but it's tomorrow night and I didn't sign up for it," I replied.

Iza stepped forward and said, "I have to drop out

because of some family get-together. My spot is open, and I asked if you could fill in for me. The director of the talent show said that would be no problem. Maybe you could sing something."

"That would be great. I love to sing. Thanks. I have to get to practice, but should I see the director first?" I asked. My heart was racing as fast as my mind. What would I sing?

Iza told me that she would let the director know, so I got my basketball clothes out of the locker and ran down to the gym.

Practice went really slow because I had something else on my mind. Even Coach Fancher noticed it and wondered what was wrong. I tried to keep my mind on the game, but I kept thinking about which one of my background tapes I would use.

After practice, I hurried home. "Mom, where are you?" I called out.

Mom stepped into the hallway. "What is it, Caitlin?"

"There is an opening in the talent show at school tomorrow night. Do you know where my background tapes are?"

"I saw them today when I was looking for something in the boxes. Which one do you want to sing?" she asked. She walked me to the family room where several boxes sat unpacked. "They're right here." She popped open a box.

"I'm going to go through each song and see which works best." I spun around and ran to my room. If I won the talent contest, everyone would forget about the curse, and I could get on with my life at Crider Middle School.

I pushed open my bedroom door with my foot because I was balancing the stack of tapes in my hands. I almost made it to the bed before the cassettes wobbled, then toppled. I was able to toss most of them onto the bed, but two fell on the floor. The plastic boxes for the tapes separated and sent the musical recordings sliding along my hardwood bedroom floor until they stopped somewhere deep under my bed.

I stretched out on my stomach and stuck my face under the bed.

I expected to find only the tapes, but I was wrong.

The first thing I saw was an old gym sock. Behind it were two yellow, beady eyes.

20

I was starting to get as angry as I was frightened.

"I've had enough, Hezekiah. If you plan on turning me into green ooze . . ." I grabbed the sock as I spoke.

I yanked, but he yanked back.

He ripped the sock from my hands. I rolled away from the bed and pushed up the sleeves on my pullover shirt. I was about to get serious.

I stuck my face under the bed again. "Listen, I want you out of my life, and I want you to take your stinking rash with you."

I grabbed for the sock again and pulled. The sock moved my way, but from the weight, I knew something else was coming with it.

I pulled with all my might but let go with one hand to grab the chair—I planned to pin him to the floor with it when he came out. With only one hand resisting him, Hezekiah pulled back farther under the bed.

Both hands gripped the sock. I pulled and rolled. It worked. The sock offered its toe from under the bed.

Another hard yank would put Mr. Bones in position to be captured. All I had to do was roll away from the bed, grab the chair, and set the legs down on both sides of him. My body weight would keep him trapped.

There was only one hitch to my plan. I had to take my eyes off the long sliver of nonhumanity for a few seconds.

Sucking in the air that I needed for strength, I rolled over and gripped the chair. Holding the sock with one hand, I swung the chair over my head to pin Hezekiah to the bedroom floor. I scurried to my feet and plopped my body on the chair before looking over toward the door and yelling, "Mom, come upstairs quick. I've captured him."

My face was already breaking into a big grin when my mom raced into my bedroom. "Mom, I've captured him."

"I see, dear. But how did you know to even look?" she asked. She had a puzzled expression on her face.

"You knew he was here and didn't tell me?" I couldn't believe it.

"I didn't know to look under your bed, but I was looking. That's why the rascal was hiding." She smiled and then bent down to get closer.

I was still too frightened to look.

Mom said, "Bad dog!"

I looked down and saw Pansy's long fur. She had gone under the bed to chew on one of my socks. I felt foolish.

"You can let her up now, Caitlin, and I'll take her downstairs. I knew she was hiding. Someone got into the kitchen garbage. I assumed it wasn't your friend Hezekiah Bones but my furry friend Pansy."

I climbed off the chair and let Pansy up. She followed my mother out the bedroom door with her head dragging low and her tail between her legs.

I grabbed my headphones, my portable cassette player, and the lost tapes that had started the tug-of-war with my imagination and lay on my bed.

I listened to each tape but chose a Renee Garcia song. I could do a killer version of that piece.

The following day, I began to get nervous about singing in the talent show. Many of the students were friendly to me, but they still kept a safe distance away from my touch. I hoped that in a few hours a win in the talent competition would cause them to forget Hezekiah Bones and the curse.

After basketball practice, I walked over to the auditorium stage. No one was in the room, and it was getting dark. The fading sun gave me enough light to keep from falling and to get a feel of the stage.

I had brought my boom box with me so I could

practice once before the talent show. New stages always made me nervous. I put the boom box on the stage and punched the play button.

As the music started I went through the first few minutes of it and was getting wound up for the big ending when the stage lights came on like lightning. I wasn't used to them, and my eyes went blind.

"Who's there?" I yelled over the music.

"I've done it again," I heard the voice say from behind me. I recognized it. Mr. Jinx entered the stage area behind me. "Once again I scared you. I usually walk in the back door and flip on the stage lights before I sweep and clean the stage. I didn't even hear your music until my finger had pushed the switch."

"That's all right, Mr. Jinx. Right now, you're probably the best friend I have in this school. Did you find out how to get rid of the curse?"

"Young lady, I've got the answer, and it is right up your alley." He beamed with joy.

"Go ahead. I can't wait to hear." I was about to hear the answer to my problems.

"All we have to do is beat Upper Darby in Tuesday night's game. If we do, Hezekiah Bones will return, and the curse will disappear," he reported.

My heart sank. The school had not beaten Upper Darby in a half century! I would be cursed for life. "We can't beat them. They're tied with us to lead the league. They've beaten everyone."

"So have the Crider Cats," Mr. Jinx reminded me. "Personally, I think you're going to beat the designer athletic shoes right off them."

"Thanks for the encouragement. Listen, I better get home so I can eat and be back for the talent show. Thanks for getting that information from your father. Tell him that I said thank you."

"I sure will, Caitlin. I hope you do well tonight," he said in an encouraging tone.

I hurried home to get ready for the evening. Mom and Dad were coming to hear me. They never missed a game, a show, or even an important day at school if they could possibly help it.

I rode with my parents to the school but left them early to hurry backstage. I checked in with the director of the talent show and found Scott.

"What are you doing here?" I asked.

"Displaying my talents in hopes to gain vast fame and fortune," he joked.

"I meant, what do you do?"

He laughed and said, "A magic show."

"I can't wait to see it." Chatting eased my nervousness.

"I'm on second, so I better finish getting the magician's costume on. I need to shove a dozen rabbits into my hat and ten pigeons up my sleeve. Would you help?" Scott said with a twinkle in his eye. His face grew serious, and then he scratched his head.

"What's wrong?" I asked.

"My black magician's cape. It was right here just before you came, and now it's not anywhere I can see," he told me. He scurried around the area. The emcee for the night had introduced the first act as Scott was still searching.

"Scott, you are onstage in two minutes. Relax and focus. You don't need a cape to be good," I counseled.

"True, but I need it to look good," he retorted. Then he smiled and finished preparing his tricks and illusions. He recovered well from the loss of his cape and pulled off his section of the show very nicely. I wasn't onstage till the end since I was the last one to sign up.

A few minutes before I was to go onstage, a loud sound of metal striking metal filled the air. It distracted the girl onstage playing her violin, and she hit a wrong note.

I moved around so I could see if anyone was up on the catwalk used to change the higher stage lighting. For a second, I was sure that I saw the corner of a black cape moving along the dark walkway.

I pointed it out to Scott, but he looked too late. "Does that mean I have to climb all the way up there to get my cape back? Or does it mean that the Phantom of the Opera has come to haunt our talent show?"

I shook my head at his silliness and was jarred

back to reality when the stage manager called for me to take my place in the stage wings.

The emcee began, "Ladies and gentlemen, our next act is new to Crider Middle School and is one of our future basketball stars. Caitlin James."

I had hoped to hear thunderous applause. Instead, I heard soft in-unison whispering of "Hezekiah, Hezekiah, Hezekiah," repeated over and over again until Dr. Wiser stood up in the first row. The room went dead silent.

The tape began, and I began singing and the kids began moving to the music. I knew I could win the talent show with the part that followed next. It was a big ending, and I had some strong notes. I started to feel the excitement building inside.

I closed my eyes to reach for that last bit of energy when the audience started screaming.

In the next second, a body hit me with a flying tackle, and I heard a loud thudding crash on the stage where I had been standing.

I opened my eyes to see that Scott was the one who had tackled me, and the director was leaning over something at my feet.

I sat up and scrambled on my hands and knees to look at what had nearly clobbered me.

It was a dummy dressed in an old black sweat suit and made from plastic foam packing material, the kind that looks like peanuts. Scott's black cape was tied around the neck of the dummy. Pinned to its chest was a dirty, graying, smelly gym sock with a message written on it:

You are cursed. Not even the
Phantom of Phys Ed can save you.

Hezekiah Bones

The teachers and principal and vice principal searched the premises and talked to kids in hopes of discovering the culprit. No one had seen anything.

The school staff got everyone seated to hear the judges' choice for the best in the talent show.

I hadn't even gotten to the good part of the song. My hopes of being accepted were crushed once again.

One of the judges, the band teacher, went onstage to announce the winner. He blew in the microphone to make sure it was on and said, "It has been difficult. Crider Middle School is filled with talented young women and men, and we've got a tie for first place.

"First place goes to Caitlin for her singing talent and to Scott for his lifesaving, death-defying leap. Let's give them both a great big hand." He handed us each trophies.

I couldn't believe it. I had won! It had been a good night except for the mysterious dummy that dropped from the catwalk and nearly cracked my head.

I turned back to take a look at the dummy sprawled on the stage. I wondered how Hezekiah Bones could have managed to do it and get away so fast.

I was carrying my trophy out to my parents' car when Kris tugged on my jacket. "Several other kids are coming to my house for a little after-the-talent-show party. It won't last long. Would you like to come?"

I turned to Mom and Dad. I didn't have to ask. They could see from my eyes how much I wanted to go. Mom broke into a smile and told us, "Sure, the winner always needs to celebrate."

When we got to Kris's house, her mom greeted us at the door. Eight of us piled into their family room where chips and soft drinks waited for us. We sank into the big overstuffed couch and chairs and talked so fast that I couldn't keep track of all the different conversations going on.

Iza called for our attention.

"I think we should toast our resident and future Grammy Award winner."

They all raised their glasses and took a drink. Scott called out, "Speech, speech."

"What can I say? This has been a crazy week. Since I came to Crider Middle School, I've gotten a curse on me, I've been chased around the school carnival by Hezekiah Bones, and I was nearly beaned by a dummy dressed as the Phantom of the Opera. Thanks for the warm and sincere welcome!" We broke into laughter.

When the giggles died down, Kris said, "Hey— let's turn the lights down really low and tell ghost stories. Who wants to go first?"

Iza sat forward. "I know one, but it isn't a story. It's true. My cousin from Toledo told me that it happened to a friend of hers."

We all groaned to register our disbelief, but it didn't deter her.

Iza started her eerie tale, but her story was stopped abruptly when the back door to the family room flew open with a crashing sound.

A ghostly figure entered the room.

Our heads snapped upward, and our bodies stiffened with fright. Through the door came a white figure. His hand clutched a long brown object.

Iza screamed.

We all joined in.

The ghostly, ghastly figure moved in our direction and raised the object in his hand.

"Fresh French bread anyone?"

Kris started laughing. "Perfect timing, big brother," she said. "I'm sorry everyone, but my big brother works at a bakery to help pay for college. He does look a lot like a ghost when he walks in with the flour all over him."

"I didn't realize that my entrance was going to cause so much excitement, but I did bring a gift of warm bread. Anyone want some?" he asked.

We all declined since it was time to go home. I lived down the block and around the corner. My house was even closer if I chose to go through the wooded empty lot that was directly between our homes.

As I walked out of the house, Kris's mom stopped me. She said that the new neighbor's dog kept breaking the chain, leaping the fence, and chasing people who passed by. She thought the two-minute run through the vacant lot would be safer.

I had not taken the pathway among the trees before, but I imagined that if I ran along the path, it would lead me to my house.

My imagination worked hard to convince me that Hezekiah Bones waited behind every tree. I tried humming one of my favorite hymns to still my imagination.

I started out at a quick run, remembering the dreams and scares and crashing catwalk dummy.

After a while, I slowed to a jog. I didn't think that the walk home should have taken so long. When I passed a half-fallen tree for the third time, I realized that the pathway must move around the wooded lot in a circle. I moved to the edge of the woods.

I took two steps. Was that a noise behind me?

I stopped and listened. The noise came again.

It sounded like a twig scratching through the dirt. I drew another breath. I had to get out of there and get out fast before Hezekiah had me in his grasp.

Since I had absolutely no idea where I was along the circle, I broke out of the trees at a run.

I skidded to a stop fast when I nearly ran into long white fangs and angry eyes only inches from my face.

23

I was facing a large collie with her teeth bared. She took two steps closer to me. I couldn't run; the dog would chase me.

She stood her ground, and I did the same. Despite my fear, I managed to notice that she was obviously well taken care of. She wasn't a stray.

She lowered her head. Her upper lip rolled back over her teeth.

I had only one thought: *If she is well groomed, she might be well trained.* Working with Pansy had taught me that a well-trained dog will respond to a clear, loud command.

The longhaired canine quickened her pace.

"Stop!" The collie froze in place. I commanded, "Sit!" And she dropped her hind legs into a sitting position. The collie's teeth went back behind the lips, and the tongue of a friendly dog flopped out of her mouth. The tail was flipping side to side in an excited wag

With my foot, I scooted a stick toward me and bounced it off the top of my shoe like a soccer ball and into my hand. Her eyes widened as she prepared herself to play.

For about five minutes I threw the stick as far as I could, and the gold-and-white collie bounded through the moonlight to fetch it.

After the sixth or seventh toss, I dropped to one knee and waited for her return. The dog walked up to me and gave me a big, sloppy dog kiss across the cheek. We had become friends, and she was one friend that wasn't afraid to touch me.

I walked her toward her owner's house. It was my plan to open the gate and put her back in. But in the dark I couldn't find it.

At the back of the fence, trees created a deep cover of darkness. The gate might have been tucked back there to discourage trespassers.

I squinted my eyes and stared as hard as I could. I couldn't see if there was a gate or not, but I was sure that I saw something move—something tall.

Most likely, my eyes were playing tricks on me. I was learning not to trust what I thought I saw.

The collie and I sneaked along the fence in the direction of the figure. I wasn't scared. If Hezekiah was standing in those trees, he would be surprised to learn I had a dog with me.

I slowed down when I was an inch or two from

the corner. I took a quiet step into the small thicket of trees.

He was standing on the other side of the trees, waiting for me with his arms outstretched.

I had my hand on the dog's collar to keep her from leaping on Hezekiah before I could tell him exactly what I thought of his curse.

The collie was showing no sign of concern over the figure in her yard. Was the dog sent to escort me into Hezekiah's hands?

One more step and I was at the edge of the thicket, taking my first look at Hezekiah Bones. He was tall with tattered clothes, and straw stuck out of each arm and his neck. His legs were two long sticks driven into the ground.

My monster was a scarecrow!

I laughed at myself and went back to my search for the gate. I was unsuccessful, and I decided I should simply go to the front door and ring the bell.

The house was the oldest in the neighborhood. The street we lived on was once a country farm, and this house was the original farmhouse. It was large and needed lots of repairs.

I climbed the stairs of the front porch. They creaked loudly. My fright-o-meter was about to peak into the red zone.

The doorbell gave off an eerie glow in the blackness of the porch. I was relieved that I could find it easily. When I stretched out my hand to ring the bell, I noticed my finger was shaking like a small limb in a windstorm. I pulled in a deep breath and settled myself.

I pushed the bell, and I could hear it ring inside. At first there was no movement, but then I heard heavy steps approaching the door. A muffled voice said something, and the door slowly opened. The second the collie saw a slight opening, she leaped against the door and bounded inside.

I had been looking down at the collie, and once she cleared out of the way, I noticed black shoes, black pants, and a white lab coat. I was not prepared for what I saw next. The neck bulged with greenish gray fish gills.

I gulped. I was afraid to look any higher, but I had to know.

Standing over me was a fish monster with green scales covering its head and two large bulging eyes.

I backed up to run, but the monster reached out one long tentacle and caught me.

I screamed.

The other long tentacle reached to its face and grabbed the scaled mouth and pulled. A mask popped off the monster's head, and two of the most gentle eyes I had ever seen were revealed.

"I'm so sorry. Did I give you a fright?" he asked.

"Yes, you did, and it was a big-time fright."

"My name is George Patterson. You're the girl at the new neighbor's house, aren't you?" he said and asked at the same time.

"Yes. I'm Caitlin James. I found your dog wandering around outside. We played a bit and then I brought her back," I told him. The tension from the fright was beginning to drain from my body. I stared at him. I wanted to ask about the monster mask but didn't. Instead, my eyes kept going from his face to his hand.

He noticed my stares and smiled. "Oh, the mask. You want to know about the mask. Can I get you a glass of lemonade?"

"No, thanks. I have to be home soon," I answered. My eyes looked past him through the door. I saw one framed horror movie poster after another stretched across the walls of the living room. There were posters from the really old black-and-white movies to the latest films.

He noticed me admiring his collection. Mr. Patterson pointed to different posters. "That one is mine and so is that one."

"What is?" I was really puzzled.

"The monster's mask was my creation. I used to make all of the horrible faces of the characters in those Hollywood classics. I did Frankenstein's monster and Wolfman." He pointed to the faces on the posters.

"Why did you quit?" I wondered.

"It was time to retire. My health isn't what it used to be, and the pressure was getting to be too much for me. My daughter needed someone to watch her kids while she worked, so, I left Hollywood and bought this house for us.

"Before I left, I told the studios that I would be glad to do a few small jobs when they needed me. I guess no one ever explained what retirement means to those movie big shots. They are sending me a new piece to do every week.

"I haven't even had time to get out and meet the neighbors. But it looks like Lassie's old stand-in, Sonny, has," he said.

"Lassie's stand-in and monster masks! That's pretty cool. I'd love to see how you make the masks sometime when I can stay.

"And I wouldn't be that concerned about getting out and meeting the people around here. They won't even come near me," I said in a woe-is-me voice.

"What's the problem?" he asked.

I told him all about the curse and how I needed to win the big, impossible game to end it. I told him how Hezekiah Bones would appear when I did it. "But that's the abbreviated story, Mr. Patterson."

He smiled and said, "Ask your folks if you can stop by tomorrow. I'll show you my work area, and you can finish the story."

The next day, Saturday, went by quickly. I met Mr. Patterson's daughter and her children, and Mr. Patterson showed me around his workroom.

I wished that my monster was as easily removed as pulling off a mask. But it wasn't that easy. If I wanted to get rid of Hezekiah, we had to win the big game on Tuesday night.

That afternoon, I ran into Scott coming out of the library just as I was going in. He'd been talking to Ben and reading about curses. He motioned me to a bench to talk.

"What did you find out?" I asked.

"A curse is saying something bad about another person or place. It is also the act of wishing something bad on another person or place. That's the simple part.

"But we still have to find out if bad things can happen to you if you are cursed by somebody else.

"From everything I read, it looks like that can't really happen. But if you believe you are cursed, you will see unrelated events that convince you that you are cursed. From that point on, the curse becomes a self-fulfilling prophecy."

"Everybody keeps saying that," I said. "But look what's happening to me—I'm not writing notes on gym socks or making people disappear or giving myself a rash!"

"Maybe there's something else going on," Scott said.

It was hard to think. A lot of crazy things were happening in my life. I wanted to have faith. I really did. But there were too many coincidences just to explain them all away.

"The big game is Tuesday night. Maybe the team can win the game and I can be done with this curse."

"We've got to win," agreed Scott.

"Or I'll never be rid of the curse."

The big story at school on Monday morning was the dummy that was thrown off the catwalk at me. Last week everyone was afraid to touch me, but after that incident at the talent show most kids wouldn't even come near me. They were afraid that the ghoul of our school would try to bean me with something and miss.

Before practice, the other players were arguing over who was going to guard me. They were afraid that something could happen to them if my body came within 10 feet of theirs. The coach got irritated because everyone stayed away from me.

"We will never beat Upper Darby if you don't play hard in practice. No one is guarding Caitlin. What is going on?" Coach Fancher asked.

I spoke up. "Coach, everyone thinks that I have the curse of Hezekiah Bones. If they touch me, they get it."

"That is the dumbest thing. All of you are in middle

school. It is time to forget about fairy tales. In fact, all of you come with me." The coach headed out of the gym and came back with a crowbar from the custodian's supply room. Coach Fancher marched us down to Hezekiah Bones's smelly locker.

"We have allowed this little charade to go on too long. I am going to open this locker, and you will see that it is filled with nothing. Nothing. That is exactly what a curse is; it is nothing."

As the coach talked, she touched her back to the locker. The team gasped.

"Someone tell me, what is supposed to happen now that I've touched the locker?" she asked.

Kris said, "Bad things will happen to you."

Mel added, "You will get a rash."

I said, "Everyone will ignore you and try to stay away."

Coach Fancher smiled at us all. "Does everyone here believe all that?"

Kris said, "I forgot to say that anyone who tells the story to another person becomes invisible for one day."

The coach laughed. "Invisible? Who became invisible?"

"Scott," I said. "He told me the story in study hall and moments later he disappeared. It was twenty-four hours before he showed up again at our study hall."

"I think it is time to see what is inside the locker," she said as she wiggled an end of the crowbar into the slit of the door.

Coach Fancher used all her strength, but nothing happened.

She asked some kids to help her, but they were afraid to touch her. I wasn't.

I walked up and put my weight against the bar. The metal creaked and groaned.

We pushed again. The metal door groaned and heaved around our crowbar. The door popped, and the very bottom left corner of the door opened just a bit.

The coach and I threw all our body weight behind the next surge of energy, and it opened a little more.

"This one will do it, Caitlin. Let's put everything we have behind this push," she told me.

The door metal bent some more. Something fell out of the bottom. It was small and pink. Before I could get close to see what treasure we had found, someone yelled, "It's a finger."

Half the team stood screaming while the other half went running for the protection of the neighboring hallway.

Coach Fancher and I leaped back a few feet. The finger continued rolling my way.

I backed as far as I could go. Was Hezekiah Bones trying to let me know what happened to his other victims? Would I turn to green ooze and watch my extremities fall off?

The finger rolled closer. I wanted to run. It came to a stop against the rubber ribbing of my high-top.

"Ahh! Somebody help me!" I yelled.

The coach pushed through the crowd of the team members. Each person she touched gasped. They were cursed. As those players backed up in an attempt to avoid me and the coach, they touched the others.

I don't even think that they saw Coach Fancher reach down and pick up the finger and hold it in the air. She smiled when she saw what it really was. She bellowed out, "Team, come over here!"

As the other players came slowly to her, I noticed they were all trying to find out who was cursed by the coach's touch and who had been touched by those kids. The coach noticed it too. She turned and winked at me.

Coach Fancher got her stern look that made her eyebrows go even across her forehead like someone drew them on with a ruler and black marker.

"This finger is merely a long, round pink eraser. I have a feeling that if we actually did get that locker open, we would find nothing. There is nothing to the curse. And all of you will see that because I touched each of you.

"If Caitlin is cursed, so are you. If I am, then you've got Hezekiah Bones breathing down your necks as well."

The eyes of my teammates grew large with fear. I wondered how Hezekiah Bones would be able to terrorize so many of us at once. Could he climb every catwalk? Could he be in every dark, empty hallway?

The coach continued talking to them. "Now, no one has to worry about getting the curse from Caitlin. We've all been touched."

"Not me," came a strong, defiant voice from the rear of the crowd. Mel was standing as far from the crowd as possible. "I figured that this is exactly what would happen. I stayed back in the other hall. I have not been touched. I am not cursed. So, everyone just stay away from me."

Coach Fancher smiled at him and said, "I'm sorry to hear that, Mel. It looks like nobody can play on the team unless he or she has been cursed. And you're too good of a player to lose . . ."

Mel's face paled. "You'll have to catch me first," he yelled and then spun around to run.

At that point, he realized Kris was right in front of him. She touched her finger to his nose and said quietly, "Surprise."

After the coach led us back to the basketball court, we had our best practice ever. If we played Upper Darby the way we had practiced, the game was in the bag.

Before I left for home, I walked down to the coach's office to thank her for doing what she did. I cleared my throat as I stood by her door.

"Caitlin, come on in. We had a great practice tonight, didn't we?" Coach Fancher said as she stuck a slice of fruit into her mouth.

"I just wanted to say thank you. Last week was difficult and lonely, but I feel like it is all behind me now," I told her.

"This curse business is getting out of hand. I'm glad that all the kids will have to deal with it. Now they'll see that there isn't any proof or substance to it."

I nodded my head in agreement. She looked at me and said, "This fruit is good. I went to college in Florida, and this stuff grew everywhere. I shouldn't eat so much, but I can't help it."

"I tried some the other day," I answered and then grinned again. "Coach, thanks. I'm really glad that you're here."

"Believe me, Caitlin, you're not as glad as I am to have you in this school and on this team," she said appreciatively.

I was sure that things were turning around for me at Crider Middle School. Even the rash from the curse was going away.

Coach Fancher sat back down at her desk, and I started to walk out. I turned to give her one last thank you when I noticed her pulling her nails across her forearm.

Was she scratching . . . ?

27

I was tired Tuesday morning. I had spent most of the night before thinking about the curse and about our chances of winning the game against Upper Darby.

Upper Darby's district poured money into the sports programs. Their gym was new, and their coach once played pro basketball.

Crider was an old school with limited financial resources, and we hadn't beaten Upper Darby since before our parents were born.

The moment I walked into the school I felt the tension and the excitement. In each class the teacher had written GO CRIDER CATS! on the chalkboard. Students talked about nothing else. The cafeteria was the noisiest that I had heard it.

All classes were canceled for the last period of the day. We were having a pep rally in the gym.

By the time I got to my locker and then into my chair at the center of the court, most of the other players were seated. Kris had saved a seat next to her. She motioned for me to take it.

"What goes on at a pep rally here?" I asked.

"The team is introduced, the principal says some nice things about us, and the coach goes up and pulls her official jacket from the box," she answered.

"Her what?"

"Her official jacket," she said. "She keeps it locked up between games. It's supposed to be lucky. When Coach Fancher removes the jacket, we have officially claimed victory against our opponent. The jacket is in our school colors—blue and green. Coach Fancher will put it on and not take it off until the end of the game."

"And it's supposed to be lucky?" I joked.

"Against every other team it has been lucky, but it has never been lucky against Upper Darby. Beating them will take something special," Kris returned. "Shhh. The program's about to start."

Kris was right about the program. After he introduced us, Dr. Wiser gave us a pep talk. Then Coach Fancher strolled up to the microphone as the students started a thunderous chant of "Go Cats!" It was deafening at first, but it filled me with a real desire to win the game.

I already knew I *had* to win it, but now I *wanted* to win it.

The coach held her arms in the air and motioned the students to quiet down. A hush descended.

"This is it, Cats! Today we beat Upper Darby!"

The screams and stomping got louder. The coach

reached under the podium and pulled out a large tattered box. The moment the kids saw it they went silent.

"Inside this box is the official Cat jacket. The moment I put it on, victory is ours. Upper Darby will meet the toughest team they've ever played and will beg us to stop scoring on them.

"The moment of truth has arrived," she told the students gathered around her.

Coach Fancher dramatically untied the string wrapped around the box and let it drop to the floor. A whoop rose among the students and then stopped.

Next, she slowly pulled the top from the box and held it high in the air. The crowd yelled, "Yes!" "Yes!"

Raising her hands, Coach Fancher calmed them down again. She reached under the paper that was wrapped around the coat and quickly yanked it out. I expected to see the coat, the symbol of our victory. Instead, she raised her hand and stared at the green ooze covering it.

In shock, the coach mumbled, "It's gone. The jacket has been stolen."

Dr. Wiser ran up next to the podium and stuck his hand into the box and removed it. Clutched in his green ooze–dripping fingers was a gym sock. From where I sat I could read the words on it:

> You are cursed.
>
> H. B.

The entire school body went stone silent. Not a movement, cough, or sneeze could be heard. The jacket had been stolen.

Dr. Wiser brushed past Coach Fancher and moved to the microphone again.

"I don't know who did this, but I can assure you that when I find out, that person will serve detention every night after school until he or she graduates."

He was furious, but I didn't think that the practical joker was sitting in the stands around us. It had to be the work of Hezekiah Bones, and he could be hiding anywhere.

Who else could have gotten into the locked locker, stolen a jacket, and filled the box with green ooze?

It looked like the coach and the team faced some strange happenings, just as I had. Hezekiah was out for us all.

The students were excused from the gym. Coach Fancher was slumped in her chair looking into the box at the green ooze. I walked up to her.

"I'm sorry that I brought the curse down on the team. How will we win without the lucky jacket?"

Coach Fancher looked at me with great surprise and said, "That's right. You don't know. I forgot to tell the team about our new player. I haven't met him yet, but he enrolled in the school today. Normally I would never allow anyone to play who hadn't even been to practice. But he was named to the All-American Middle School All-Star Team last year, and I think we need him.

"We'll win this game. With Mel and you and our new all-star playing, Upper Darby doesn't have a chance."

The coach leaped from her seat and headed for her office. She had to prepare the team for the big game.

I gazed at the empty gymnasium. In a few hours, it would be full of cheering fans from Crider Middle School who needed a victory.

Mom and Dad picked me up at school, and we went out to eat. Ben met us at the restaurant. It was our little tradition before a game.

Dad said the blessing before the meal and asked God to help me play a good game. I didn't eat much, but it was nice to get away from the distractions and things to do at home or school.

Dad reached across the table and asked, "Caitlin, what's wrong? You're acting as if you saw a ghost today. Is it this Hezekiah Bones thing your mom told me about?"

Dad did not believe in ghosts and such any more than Mom or Ben. Prior to attending Crider, I hadn't, either. I kept trying to line up what was happening to me with what I knew to be true about Jesus and his protection. But my faith was still letting me down.

I looked at Dad and said, "I told you and Mom that Coach Fancher touched the locker. Today at the pep rally, when she was about to pull her official jacket from its box, she discovered the coat was missing and the box was filled with green ooze.

"It's the kind of coat that is worn only for games, and it's kept locked away so no one could take it. I'm sure that Hezekiah Bones is involved with it. If we don't win the game tonight . . ."

After dinner, I ran out first to unlock the car doors. As I inserted the key, I glimpsed an extremely tall kid standing only a few feet away.

In the dim light of the evening, I couldn't make out his face, but I didn't have to.

I knew who it was.

29

He disappeared as quickly as he had appeared. He was making one more attempt to intimidate me before the big game.

I was more determined than ever for the Crider Cats to win that game.

When we arrived at the school, I changed and joined the team. The coach gathered us in the weight-lifting room for a pep talk.

"Tonight is our biggest game. Once we get past Upper Darby, it is straight on to the championship. We can win this game. We have the best players in the conference, and tonight we're adding a new one. I haven't met him, but he was an all-star player for his former team. We have everything we need to do it. Now, get out there and do the job."

As we jogged out to the gym, I breathed a quick prayer for strength and stamina to do what we needed. By the time we hit the gym floor, the stands were filled with noisy students.

The Upper Darby team went through their drills, and I watched. They were good. They were very good. But I knew that we had good players.

Coach Fancher was still looking for our new player as the game began. Mel and I passed the ball back and forth and scored on most of our possessions, but Upper Darby kept pace with us.

The minutes of the first half ticked by. When the buzzer sounded, we were tied at 25 points each.

Our halftime rest was filled with silence. I could not believe how good the Upper Darby team could play. They were not making it easy. As we rested, Coach Fancher stood by the door waiting for the new player.

Halftime passed, but no all-star joined the roster.

We started the next half with the seesawing score continuing. My jump shots were on.

Our Crider team was playing well but not well enough to finally take the lead. Upper Darby was getting around us with layups.

Their team pulled into the lead. At first it was two points and then four. A foul shot put them up by five.

The coach called a time-out, and we headed for the bench.

"There are three minutes left. We need to pull that five-point gap down. Caitlin's jump shot has been our biggest gun. Feed her for the next minute."

The team did as the coach said, but my scoring ran dry. For the next minute I shot five times and scored nothing. The only thing that kept us in the game was Upper Darby's inability to score as well.

The two-minute warning sounded. As I trotted back to the bench, the students began chanting, "Caitlin has a curse. No one could play worse." I felt miserable.

In our huddle the other players looked at me. Mel was the first to speak. "We're losing because of you and the curse that's on the whole team."

"If there really is a curse of Hezekiah Bones, he'd better show his face tonight. Look around you. Do you see a skinny giant anywhere in this building?"

Suddenly, in the silence of the hometown audience, the back double metal doors banged open. A silhouette appeared in the doorway. It was a very tall and gaunt young man. Not one of us was mistaken about the figure's identity.

The last stage of the curse was about to begin. Hezekiah Bones had come to drag me away.

30

The students in the stands had seen what we had.
They began moving quickly to the exit doors.

Coach Fancher grabbed her bullhorn. "Students,
please be calm."

She found it difficult to settle them down as the tall
figure stepped into the gym's light and started across
the floor. The extra tall boy was dressed in our basketball uniform, but it was small on him.

I searched the stands, looking for a hiding place or
a route of escape. I backed up slowly. Several hands
from my teammates gripped me and shoved me back
in the direction of Hezekiah Bones.

I had little choice.

The coach saw me trying to slip away and grabbed
my arm. She spoke into her bullhorn again.

"Students, this is our newest player for the team,"
she yelled into the voice amplifier.

I was surprised that it actually worked. Everyone
stopped and took a long look at the tall, thin boy

headed our way. He had a friendly face. He was not a monster. Murmurs of conversation drifted together, and the fans returned to their seats.

Our new teammate moved to the bench.

He smiled at us and said, "Sorry I'm so late, but we had some car problems on the way. Where do we stand?"

"There are two minutes to go, and we're behind by five points," I let him know. Then I said, "I'm Caitlin and you have no idea how glad I am to meet you. What's your name?"

"They call me Hoops Bonet," he answered.

"You must be the nephew that the substitute teacher was talking about last week," I said.

The other team members watched us and moved closer to hear our conversation. They still weren't sure that he wasn't Hezekiah.

The referee approached our bench. "Coach, I'm going to give your team another 30 seconds and then start the game again with two minutes to go."

Coach Fancher looked at us all. "We need five points fast. Hoops, stay near their basket. Every time they throw up a shot, grab the ball out of the air, and toss it full court to Caitlin. She will stay down by our basket. She'll have easy, clear shots.

"Remember, we need three of those shots in two minutes. Mel and the rest of you, make Upper Darby cough up the ball when they have it."

We headed to the court. I was tall, but standing next to Hoops made me look and feel like a midget. He was big, and that was exactly what we needed.

Upper Darby inbounded the ball and drove to their basket. Hoops had already taken a few leaps toward their basket. When the Upper Darby player tossed the ball at the rim, Hoops put his hands in the air and snagged it. The Upper Darby shooter stopped in midrun. He was shocked.

The next play truly surprised our opponents. I was waiting under our basket as Hoops's pass floated gracefully in the air. I grabbed it, took a good look at the net, and popped it in. We were down by only three.

Upper Darby maneuvered the ball around the backcourt in hopes of getting a player behind Hoops for a layup. Mel broke through and stole the ball but was moving down the hardwood floor so fast that he could not make the cut away from the sideline. Moments before he went out of bounds, Mel pitched the ball blindly behind him.

Upper Darby caught it. They moved it around, running down as much clock time as they could. The shot clock ticked away until they had to shoot again, but Hoops's big hands snagged the ball from the air and tossed it to me. I shot, and we were one point behind.

Only thirty seconds were left on the time clock. If

we could get the ball quickly and shoot, they would have the last possession. We would be better off to allow them to run the clock down and then get the ball.

That was exactly what happened. Two of Upper Darby's players passed the ball back and forth in hopes of finding an open shot around Hoops.

They concentrated so hard on Hoops that Kris dived in and knocked the ball free. Mel scooped the ball up from the floor and spun. He had to make a long throw to reach me, but if he did, we would win the game.

The pass flew into the air and sailed at me. I could tell it would be short, but the bounce would have it in my range. The Upper Darby team figured that out as well. Two of their biggest players were steaming down on me at top speed. Once the ball made it to my hands, I would have only enough time to turn and shoot. I had to forget about the luxury of taking a good look at the hoop.

The ball smacked the floor and careened into the air. I snatched the ball with my two opponents only two feet from me. One sailed into the air, and the other dived for the ball.

I didn't think. I reacted and sent the ball back into the air. It hung like a satellite in orbit. I knew people were screaming, but the only thing I heard was my heart thumping in my chest.

The ball and the backboard met. The ball moved at the rim and then proceeded to go around it once, then twice, then a third time.

The whole gym went silent.

The ball could fall either way.

31

Two large shoes smacked the polished wood floor. I turned to see Hoops leaping from the foul line. He seemed airborne. His body sailed until his fingertip could touch the ball. He tapped it at the moment the buzzer sounded. Before the buzzer ended, the ball dropped through.

We had won the game! The curse was over.

Everyone cheered loudly. I thought the roof was going to come off. Teachers and school administrators joined us on the floor. I saw Miss Wiley, the vice principal, jumping and smiling. Mr. Jinx, who was right next to her, gave me the thumbs-up sign.

After all the congratulations, our team headed for the lockers. As we approached the doors to go downstairs, a figure slipped out of the dark corner.

He was tall, very tall. He was more ghoulish than I even imagined him. It had to be Hezekiah Bones because he held Coach Fancher's lucky jacket in his hands.

We all moved back against the wall as he took a step toward us.

Miss Wiley started shouting. "This is impossible. There is no such thing as Hezekiah Bones. Mr. Jinx, how did he get the jacket? I thought you had hidden it."

We were stunned. What was she talking about?

But we had more surprises in store.

Hezekiah Bones reached up and ripped a mask from his face. It was Mr. Bonet, the substitute teacher.

Coach Fancher stepped forward. "Will someone please tell us what is going on?"

Mr. Bonet began talking. "It's a long story, but the person you call Hezekiah Bones was my grandfather. Part of the story is true, but much of it has gotten distorted over the years.

"My grandfather's real name was Jedekiah Bonet. He did play basketball here, and he did disappear in the middle of a game with Upper Darby. When he went to the locker room, his appendix ruptured, and his parents rushed him to the hospital.

"The team lost to Upper Darby, and Jedekiah's embarrassment was so great that he refused to return to this school. He did not even come back to clean out his locker.

"Over the years, the rumor developed. Just before my grandfather died, he asked that I come back here and tell everyone what really happened.

"My sister, who is Hoops's mother, and I liked the area so much on one of our visits that we decided to move here," he finished his explanation.

I was still confused. "Who was the person who haunted me and tried to drop a dummy on me?"

Mr. Bonet strolled toward Miss Wiley and Mr. Jinx. "When I first came here, I heard that you had been cursed, Caitlin. Since I knew the true story, I figured that someone was keeping the curse alive. I wanted to know why, and I asked Mr. Patterson to make me this mask to startle that person into revealing his or her identity. Tell them, Miss Wiley."

She stammered and then said, "The . . . the board was going to shut down the school. I got them to agree to keep Crider open if we won this game. I remembered the rumors about Hezekiah Bones and thought we could use the story of the curse to motivate us to win. Mr. Jinx and I planned just about every one of the pranks—including the rotten odor and the gooey green ooze that we bought at a novelty store."

"And Mel did the rest—including the stink bomb and the gym-sock warnings and the catwalk dummy," Scott said from the doorway.

"But that doesn't explain the rash or your turning invisible," said Kris.

"Those two are tied together. It's Iza's fault that Caitlin—and I—got the rash," Scott said.

"You had the rash too?" I exclaimed.

"When that stink bomb went off in the auditorium, I noticed my arms were breaking out in a rash and my lips were swelling. So after I went back to get the stuff I had left under the seat, I decided to go to the nurse before it got worse. The nurse didn't know what was causing the rash, so she suggested that time at home might be a good idea," he said.

"I never turned invisible—I simply stayed at home. But here is the important part. My family doctor figured out that my rash was an allergic reaction to the mango that Iza had given us at lunch. The mango is a member of the poison ivy family. Lots of people are allergic to it. They develop a rash and sometimes their lips swell," he said.

"So Hezekiah Bones doesn't exist?" I asked. I turned to Mr. Bonet. "But how did you get the official jacket?"

"That was easy. As I was walking to class, I saw Mr. Jinx hurrying in the other direction. The jacket was stuffed under his arm and almost hidden, but a sleeve dangled out in the back. I simply followed to see what he was going to do with it."

"So there's no Hezekiah, no curse, and nothing to be afraid of," I said. "And we won even without the official jacket."

"Correct," Mr. Bonet said.

"But because I thought that I had a curse that could

only be removed if we won, I pushed hard to help win the game, thus saving the school?" I continued.

Miss Wiley stepped forward. "I'm sorry I frightened you and the other kids, Caitlin. I only wanted the school to stay open."

Mr. Jinx stood next to her and said, "Ditto."

I smiled my acceptance of their apology. What a way to start in a new school. As soon as I could, I would have to have a little talk with Jesus and ask him to forgive me for doubting him so much. He had been with me all along. Why, he'd even helped our team win the basketball game!

"Is anybody in the mood for a celebration? Pizza without mangoes is on me," Miss Wiley announced.

I looked at Coach Fancher. "When you think of it, a school with its own Phantom of Phys Ed is pretty cool."

Coach Fancher looked at me and winked.

Read and collect all of
Fred E. Katz's

SPINE CHILLERS™

Don't miss

Not a Creature
Was Stirring?

Turn the page for a spine-chilling preview . . .

1

"I can't believe it. I just can't believe it! Why me? Why now?" I yelled the whole way back from the hospital. I wasn't usually such a crybaby, and my parents didn't let me get away with self-pity often. But this was a big disappointment for me, Conner Morgan.

My folks had been invited to speak at a marriage-counseling conference and were going to take me skiing afterward. Now I couldn't go. Why did I have to break my leg?

Ever since the summer, Dad had been promising to take me skiing the week before Christmas. I love to ski. I love having the cold air blowing against my face as I hurtle down the mountainside.

Now because of the broken leg, I couldn't go.

It all happened on the last day of school before Christmas vacation. I was in the gym practicing for gymnastics. A friend and I were doing challenges. He would do something and then I would have to try it. Then I would do something and he would have to try it.

The difference is, my friend is a little better and a little more daring.

He tried a special routine on the rings. I went behind him and completely blew it.

I climbed onto the uneven bars for my challenge. I started by swinging my midsection over the low bar and circling it. I was hotdogging and I knew it. If I wanted to win the challenge, I had to do something he couldn't do.

Next I did a handstand on the high bar, then dropped into a somersault around the low one. I looked good as I went back to the high bar.

The dismount was next. I let go of the bar and did a double somersault in midair.

I looked really good. I forgot to keep my focus and instead started thinking how my friend's eyes were probably wide open in awe.

My distraction was my downfall. Literally.

I was too close to the floor as I came out of the last head-over-heels turn.

C-r-a-c-k . . .

The pain didn't take long to hit my brain. I knew right then my leg was broken. The ski trip!

When Dad and Mom got to the hospital, I grabbed Dad's arm and begged, "Don't leave me here!"

Dad looked touched. He squeezed my shoulder. "Son, we're not leaving you. The doctor said you can go home today."

"No!" I said, realizing he misunderstood. "I'm not afraid of the hospital. I mean, don't leave me at home. Can I still go on the ski trip?"

"Conner, I know you were looking forward to this trip," Mom said, "but you wouldn't enjoy watching TV in a hotel room all day. And we wouldn't be comfortable leaving you by yourself in a town we don't know. Aunt Bergen was already coming to watch the house. With you here, now she can keep an eye on you too."

"We don't think this trip is for you, Conner," Dad said. "There will be other ski trips."

"Now, how about our getting you home?" Mom said.

When we got to the house, I sat in the living room among the Christmas tree and the decorations.

I looked at the tabletop nativity scene. It had been in my mom's family since she was a little girl. Every year we carefully placed the porcelain figurines on the table and reflected on the true meaning of Christmas.

I had always felt happy at Christmas. Until now. Every time I saw Mom or Dad carrying down a suitcase, I felt as though someone punched me in the stomach.

It was going to be a great trip, and I had to miss it. But that wasn't the worst of it.

Mom was in the kitchen getting out plates for the pizza. I called out, "Mom, since I've got to stay home, then your aunt doesn't have to come and stay in the house, right?"

She dried her hands as she walked in. "Wrong. I couldn't leave you here all alone.

"I feel okay about leaving you only because I know that Aunt Bergen will be here with you."

"Mom, I don't even know her. I've never seen her, and I would rather not have a stranger around while I'm trying to heal my broken leg."

Mom gave me a big smile. My appeal hadn't worked.

She perched on the arm of my easy chair and leaned against the back.

"This is tough for you, isn't it?" she asked, slipping a strand of hair from my eyes. "I can remember missing a horse show when I was a girl because I broke my arm. Not fun. But the Great Physician took care of me then and he'll take care of you now. You won't be lonely with him at your side.

"Besides, Aunt Bergen could use a little family around during this holiday. She's out of this world, and you will have the time of your life. She used to take care of my brother and me when we were kids. We had such a crazy time; we never knew for sure what she was up to. She used to kill us," Mom told me.

Mom continued. "I've never known anyone else quite like her. She and Uncle Charlie traveled all over the world."

She turned and left. When the doorbell rang, it took me a few minutes, but I hobbled to the front door.

I turned the doorknob and expected to see Dad's happy face smiling at me from behind a bunch of suitcases.

Instead, a flash of red and white smashed into my body and sent me flying backward.

Santa Claus? His red suit and red hat pushed through the doorway, and an inflatable Santa plastered me against the wall.

From behind Santa, Dad's big hand reached out to grab me.

"Hold it, Conner. I don't want you to fall and break another bone," Dad said.

I sighed with relief, but before I could straighten up I saw a face peering out of a black hood. The body that belonged to that face grabbed me in a bear hug.

"So this is Conner. Young man, you look just like your grandfather did at this age. The spitting image!" She flipped her hood off, and I could see her straight gray hair pulled back in a bun. It was attached by a large comb decorated in tiny faces that changed expressions when she moved. Her eyes looked at me and sparkled.

"Aunt Bergen!" Mom exclaimed as she entered the room. Aunt Bergen's arm shot out and quickly embraced Mom with a firm hug.

"Oh, my. You are all grown up. I always knew that my favorite great-niece would turn out well. And your son, Conner, is absolutely delightful," Aunt Bergen said. Her words flowed rapidly. "Now, how can I help?"

"Just knowing that you'll be here with Conner is enough," Mom said with a big smile. "Let me get you settled in the spare bedroom."

When they left, I hobbled back into the living room to keep out of everyone's way.

The evening was filled with packing and chattering. I wasn't in the mood to share in their joy. Sure, I'd been taught Colossians 1:24 and knew to "be happy in my sufferings." But I wasn't doing a very good job of it. I think everybody understood when I went to bed without saying goodnight.

By the time I was out of bed the next morning, all the luggage was waiting in the entry hall. In a few minutes we would be saying good-bye. I had always thought it would be fun to have the house to myself. But suddenly I felt very alone.

Alone. Alone with Aunt Bergen. It doesn't seem fair. It'll be the loneliest Christmas ever.

When the airport van arrived a few minutes later, Dad carried the luggage out to the curb.

Mom stayed back to hug me. She whispered, "Aunt Bergen is even crazier than I remember. There is something that you need to know about her. She is—"

Dad stepped back inside and broke in right in the

136

middle of Mom's sentence. "We'd better hurry if we're going to get to our plane in time."

"What do I need to know, Mom?" I asked, but Mom was already grabbing her gloves and running toward the door.

She said, "I'll have to tell you when I get back." She turned and went out the door, but before she stepped onto the porch she turned back to me.

She had a serious look on her face. "Watch out! Not everything is as it seems. Aunt Bergen is not quite like everyone else."

By the time I got to the door, Mom had already stepped into the van.

What did she mean when she said that Aunt Bergen was not quite like everyone else? When she said that Aunt Bergen was 'out of this world' did she mean that Aunt Bergen is some sort of alien?

The van exited the driveway and headed to the airport. I turned slowly on my cast and crutches to make my way into my parents' bedroom. That's where I'd be spending the next few days.

I came face-to-face with Aunt Bergen.

"I've got a glass of milk for you. A growing boy with broken bones needs one of these several times a day," she said as she smiled at me. All I could do was smile back. She put it in the bedroom and I followed her in.

"Isn't this a wonderful time of the year?" Aunt Bergen's voice danced with happiness.

"I suppose for some other kids it might be," I responded with a Scrooge voice.

"Do I hear a bit of 'Bah, humbug' in your voice? What would a kid not like about Christmas?" she asked.

"Don't get me wrong, Aunt Bergen, I like presents as much as the next guy, but that seems to be all people think about."

"You think so?" Aunt Bergen's eyes were twinkling, but I could tell she was taking me seriously. "Go on."

"Every year I see my mom work hard trying to make Christmas special for Dad and me. If she isn't at the malls shopping, she's in the kitchen cooking. I wish it were different. I wish . . ."

"Yes?" she prompted.

"I wish we'd take the food and presents to somebody who maybe can't afford to buy them," I said. I couldn't believe I was saying all this. I didn't know Aunt Bergen, but I felt I could tell her what was on my mind.

"Ah," Aunt Bergen said at last. "So Conner turned out just like his mom. Sounds like you appreciate all your mother does for you, and it sounds like she still puts others first before herself.

"Do you know what your mother used to do when she was a girl? She always saved some of her Christmas toys for the little girl at church whose father was killed in a car wreck. She said she didn't like having so much when her friend had so little.

"I don't think your mother has changed much," she said with a smile. "Here it is the week before Christmas and your folks are at a marriage conference helping others when they'd really like to be here with you. I guess Christmas gifts come in all shapes and sizes. And the best ones are the gifts you give of yourself."

She chucked me on the chin. "Go ahead and drink your milk, honey. I have a feeling you're going to like this Christmas after all—broken leg or no broken leg."

She disappeared down the hall, leaving me alone with the milk and my thoughts.

I climbed into bed for a nap. Had my mother really given her brand-new Christmas toys away when she was my age? And was I being too hard on my parents for leaving me alone with Aunt Bergen? Questions ran through my mind as I drifted off to sleep.

I was deep in sleep when I heard a faint tapping at my door. I wasn't sure if it was in my dream or really happening. I knew only one way to find out.

I went to the door and listened for the tapping again. What could be there? I twisted the knob and pulled the door open. My eyes flicked up and I jumped back in terror.

A ghastly green face! I stifled a scream.

Whatever it was, it was staring right at me.

SPINECHILLERS™

The week before Christmas, while Conner's family is preparing for a skiing vacation in Colorado, Conner breaks his leg. Fortunately, Great-Aunt Bergen is coming to watch the house, and Conner can stay with her. But there is something very strange about Aunt Bergen, and strange things start to happen when she arrives.

It's too late to run in . . .

Not a Creature Was Stirring?

SpineChillers™ #6
by Fred E. Katz